SIMULUMIS

LEVEL ONE

by BO MANDOE

Simulumis Level One

Copyright © 2022

by Bo Mandoe

All Rights Reserved

923 Publishing

ISBN: 9798988122906

This book is dedicated to Eva Mandoe.
May you always flow with the rhythms.

TABLE OF CONTENTS

Dedication	iii
Table of Contents	v
Chapter 1: History	1
Chapter 2: Quest	18
Chapter 3: Subversive	29
Chapter 4: The Island	52
Chapter 5: Resurrection	58
Chapter 6: Arthur's Tale	70
Chapter 7: Theory	78
Chapter 8: Council	99
Chapter 9: Marooned	108
Chapter 10: The Sibyl's Tale	124
Chapter 11: Down The River	133
Chapter 12: Coliseum	142
Chapter 13: Deuced Machine	151
Epilogue	154
Acknowledgements	161

CHAPTER 1

HISTORY

"Who can tell me the single most important factor that led to the Great Interruption?" asked Drew Dennison's teacher, Mr. Roberts, his baldheaded avatar scowling as he surveyed the roomful of kids.

Drew fidgeted in his seat and stared at his desk. He wasn't really there, of course – nobody was. There wasn't even a there, technically. The class was nothing but a glorified chat room he and his fellow students were forced to attend for three hours a day until they turned eighteen. Still, the illusion was so good that he could actually feel the hardwood seat riding up against the back of his legs, hear the soft hum of an air conditioner, and even smell the stress sweat wafting off his adolescent classmates. He may have contributed to the odor himself.

"The pandemics," someone said. Mr. Roberts wrote it on the retro chalkboard.

"War," said someone else. The word joined the first.

"Climate change."

"Competition for resources."

"Capitalism."

The list grew. Finally the answers dwindled and Mr. Roberts faced the class, obviously unsatisfied. "These are good answers," he said, "but none of them are the single most important one. Anybody else willing to give it a try? Sera? Levi? Andrew? We haven't heard from any of you yet."

Drew scowled. He hated being called on in class, especially when he didn't know the answer, which was most of the time. Maybe one of the others would get it first. He risked a glance at his friend Levi.

Levi Rosen was what would've been called a savant a hundred years ago. He had an encyclopedic memory, took everything literally, and had a very short fuse. Now it appeared that something Mr. Roberts said had set him off. His pallid complexion had grown flushed and red. He was tapping his fingers on his knees in quick succession. "It's a poorly worded question," he burst out, "are you talking about social or environmental factors? And in any case how are we supposed to address them as if they existed in a vacuum? They didn't! History is a complex fabric of interwoven events and intentions, none of which are understood in full by the people who write it. You might as well say the most important factor was complexity itself!" He broke off, breathing heavily, glaring at Mr. Roberts' avatar.

SIMULUMIS

The teacher began a slow clap. "Precisely," he said, "complexity caused the Great Interruption." A hush settled over the class. Things had gone in an unexpected direction. "Think about it," said the teacher, reverting to lecture mode, "the Industrial Revolution, the Cultural Revolution, the Digital Revolution, the Social Revolution. Telephones, automobiles, airplanes, computers, social media. So much change in such a short time. People couldn't keep up. All these other factors." He pointed at the board. "It was information warfare. People literally didn't know what was real anymore. And then they hit a bottleneck."

Flabs and Crabs, the bully twins, chortled at the image. Drew couldn't remember ever calling them anything else, but that might have been a system feature – for all Drew knew they were unaware of their own nicknames. One dropped a sound effect, a glass bottle being broken.

Mr. Roberts ignored it. "Systems require maintenance," he said, "and maintenance requires technicians, and technicians require education. The old millennials failed to maintain the sufficiently educated populace required to keep their society's infrastructure up and running. Can anybody tell me why this happened?"

"They thought robots would do it." That was Sera, speaking in a bored monotone. Drew suspected she was not actually bored but just impatient with the lesson, and had answered to keep Mr. Roberts talking. That he'd gained such an insight wasn't a comment on Drew's powers of observation so much as the sheer volume he'd focused on the stoic girl.

"That is correct," Mr. Roberts was saying, "but robots require maintenance too, and even though they built robots to maintain those robots, they also needed robots to maintain the maintenance robots, which in turn needed maintenance as well. In short, they weren't able to make a self-perpetuating society of mechanical servants. And so eventually it broke down.

"This is an over-simplification, of course," Mr. Roberts continued, "every model is. But it's useful in that it helps me illustrate a point: there's no such thing as a closed system. Not even the world we live in today. And that's why it's so important to take your education seriously. What you bring to the system will affect its rhythms for generations."

"Rhythms," Levi repeated, a frustrated look on his puffy face. "You mean algorithms."

"A fortunate piece of wordplay," Mr. Roberts observed.

"I don't get it," Sera said flatly. "Okay, so things fell apart. Why did it take so long to fix them? Why did it take twenty years and six billion dead people just to turn the internet back on?"

"Yeah," Crabs called out, "and why would anyone be crazy enough to want to turn it off again?"

"Stupid Loomie cultists!" Flabs sneered for good measure.

Mr. Roberts cut off their microphones, but the damage was done. Everyone was staring at Drew to see how he'd react. He tried to keep his face emotionless, but it was hard with all their eyes prying into him.

"Leave Mr. Dennison be," said Mr. Roberts, his voice a deadly shade of calm. "He did not ask for this burden. Please remember, when someone is hurting-"

Drew's vision blurred and the sounds around him faded. He was dissociating, and whether the virtual reality goggles he – like all the others – wore was contributing to the state he couldn't have said. It wouldn't have occurred to him that they might be purposely shielding him from the laughter at his expense. He'd worn the goggles for every moment of his life.

Well, almost.

One day when he was five years old his father had taken them off. Drew didn't remember much about the man himself, but he could recall in vivid detail the fifty-six minutes he'd spent in actual reality. He still had nightmares of that dingy, unpainted bedroom, its barren walls and the tattered mattress pad he'd sat on the edge of until two drones that looked like bumblebees came and took his father away. Then his mother had set his goggles back in place and cried over him and promised he would never be traumatized like that again.

"Why did they take Daddy," he'd asked, "why did they fly him away?"

His mother wrapped him tightly in her arms. "Your father is very sick," she explained.

"They're going to make him better again?"

But she'd just held him and cried.

#

The moment class ended Drew exited the module to reorient himself in his physical body. He chose his favorite filter, the same one he'd used every day for the last ten years. He was lying in bed, a plush double mattress on a vintage black Ikea particle board frame. His walls were adorned with pictures of fantastic creatures he'd fought in battle and pictures of even more fantastic warrior princesses he'd like to fight alongside. Or something. He was just waking up to the existence of this ineffable *more* there was to girls, but despite the extensive scrutiny directed toward his classmate he didn't really have a sense of what he was supposed to do about any of it.

Levi's avatar pinged him. "Hail, Drew the Thief! Might I interest you in an afternoon quest?"

Two years older than Drew, Levi was in his final year of school but had the social maturity of a twelve-year old. They'd made friends in the quest filter and their entire relationship was built around it. The larger youth had become a mentor of sorts, helping Drew navigate the rougher aspects of gaming, and he'd reciprocated by being friendly when nobody else would. He was the Laurel to Levi's Hardy, the George to his Lenny, the Gimli to his Legolas. He wasn't sure about that last one, or any of them honestly. Analogies, especially regarding pre-GI culture, were Levi's forte.

Truth of the matter was, nobody was being especially friendly toward Drew either.

"Hail, Lord Leviathan!" Drew leapt to his feet. "I'm ready when you are."

Lord Leviathan took a moment to respond. "Give me ten minutes. I'm, ah, cleansing the royal bowels."

"Take as long as you need. You'll still be full of crap." Drew cut the connection before Levi could respond.

#

His mother pinged him, her avatar's smile friendly and wide, its skin default yellow. She always wanted to know how his day had gone. Like one was different from another.

Sure enough. "Hi honey, how was school?"

Drew flopped back onto his bed. She could have walked down the hall and spoken to him in person. But then he could've too. "Fine."

Her eyes narrowed as she scanned his feed, surveying the dim lighting, the posters on the wall, the vibe of his teenage man cave. "That's what you always say."

Drew looked away. "They teased me about dad again."

"Oh, honey." She pouted sympathetically. "You just ignore those turkeys. Their charisma scores will suffer, see if they don't."

"It's their dexterity I'm worried about."

She pouted again. "Isn't that why you do all that questing? I'd think you were invincible by now."

"That's not how it works," Drew began, but thought better of it. Either she already understood video game economics or she never would, and it didn't really matter. You could get along just fine in life either way. If you wanted to be elite it was another story, but that was not something anyone had ever accused his mother of. She'd built a routine and was content with it, and who was Drew to tell her different? "I have to go. I'm meeting Levi for a quest."

His mother's pout turned to a frown. "Why don't you invite your friend over? Play a board game or something? I could join you."

Drew tried his very best not to cringe. "Thanks mom. Maybe next time."

She did a less than stellar job of hiding her disappointment. "Well then I'd like you to quest outside. Go play in the street or something."

#

Drew's goggles activated the common filter the moment he stepped out of the house. This meant he was viewing

SIMULUMIS

reality overlaid with certain enhancements, including those that depicted people how they wanted to be seen. Glistening joggers and ultra-motivated power walkers lined the grassy street. A china doll pulled weeds in her garden. It was a brilliant spring afternoon. The pancake sun blazed in the western quadrant of the sky and birds sang as they flitted about. The houses in Drew's neighborhood, just north of Sylvan's Gulch on the east side of the Willamette River, popped with brightly painted colors and welcoming décor. From the south came the tooting of the daily cargo train and the roar of couriers and freelance opportunists looking for a score, or at least a job delivering someone else's score to them.

This was all fairly normal. Like everyone in the 22nd century, Drew could select from over a thousand premade filters that would alter his appearance to suit his preferences – or other people's. Anyone he came across could be running a filter that changed the gender of his avatar, or the color of his skin, or any of the characteristics people used to judge each other by. It didn't bother him. That was how they got along, how they could all have nice things.

At the lowest point of the Great Interruption, when humanity was literally facing an extinction level event, the only thing everyone could agree upon was that nobody trusted anyone else to write the code for the new internet, because whoever built the language controlled the algorithms, and thereby held power over everyone else. A consortium of the brightest minds from around the world had gathered to tackle the problem, every remaining government and super corporation represented, the old line between public and private enterprise long rendered meaningless. Out of this congress came the largest gaming engine ever created, a worldwide MMORPG (massively multiplayer online role playing game) that transcended every system of government and economics humanity had ever dreamt up.

This was the history Drew learned, as had his parents before him and their parents before them. World peace hadn't come in the form of forcible globalization or fascism or any of the dystopias or utopias their ancestors had imagined. There wasn't a monoculture everyone was made to adhere to. Instead people were allowed to live out their fantasies, the simulation's game engine veiling all the differences that used to cause contention and strife.

#

Drew scrolled past the race and decency filters to the entertainment genres and selected Quest 83. The afternoon transformed into gleaming twilight and all the houses disappeared, replaced by thick forest. If he'd had a mirror he could've watched his diminutive form turn elven and his cloak blend into the waning rays of the sun. He was a Thief, albeit a low-level one. This wasn't to say he actually *stole* things. It was more like he identified with that class of player, someone who skulked in the shadows and saw things others didn't.

Not that he'd ever seen anything out of the ordinary. Nothing, that is, beyond those fifty-six minutes of harsh reality. But they were etched into his mind like a post-tribal tattoo. Or post traumatic stress.

Leviathan materialized beside him. His friend's avatar resembled his actual self in largeness and expression, but where the human was mostly fat with a little muscle around his jowls his avatar was the exact opposite. He wielded spiked gauntlets and a club and wore a comedic white toga. He grinned at Drew. "Hulk smash!"

Drew rolled his eyes. "What's our objective? Storm the castle, save the princess?" He drew his short sword. "I'd rather not use magic if we don't have to."

"Don't' need it." Leviathan sent his club on an experimental swing over Drew's head. "As far as I know we're supposed to defeat the Troll King. The intro was a little vague about our actual mission."

"Not like it's going to be that different," Drew mused. "This isn't Quest 100 or anything."

"Numerical bias." Leviathan shook his head. "Whatever. Let's get this party started."

They advanced carefully down the wooded path that was actually the street. Now the joggers resembled passing forest elves and the weeding china doll was a wart-nosed witch tending mushrooms. Carrion birds swooped through the forest canopy.

After a while the adventurers came to a recessed clearing surrounded by sloping dirt edges, like dykes to hold water in, but the bottom was dry and barren. On the far side a series of crumbling buildings gave off an apocalyptic aura.

"Troll King," Leviathan muttered. "That could mean anything. This could be cyber punk. We should have guns!"

Drew laid a hand on his friend's arm. "We've got this. The rhythm never gives us more than we can handle."

"I hate that abbreviation."

They set out stealthily across the recessed plateau, Drew bringing up the rear. For the briefest of moments he cycled back to the common filter. It kind of defeated the illusion of the quest, but you could never be too safe. Not everybody was playing the same game.

Today, however, the common filter was a literal walk in the park. Groups of kids threw virtual Frisbees while younger kids played Mario Hopscotch, their cartoon avatars bouncing wildly down the paths. Older kids huddled together in disdain, stuck in limbo between the death of imagination and common sense. On the fringe prowled questers like themselves bearing antiquated maps that read 'here be dragons.' Nothing seemed wildly out of place, so Drew switched back to quest mode.

They reached the far side and climbed the embankment. From that vantage point they could see straight into the

Troll King's fortress. It had amassed an army of Non-Player Characters that rendered it virtually untouchable to a low-level player like himself. Untouchable, that is, without a giant to lead the way. Which meant Leviathan would get all the credit, as usual.

Or maybe not! Maybe this was the perfect opportunity for a Thief to prove his quality.

Drew made his plan. He'd wrap his cloak around himself and cast a camouflage spell, his request to not use magic be damned. With any luck it would fool enough of the NPC guards for him to slip by unannounced. He'd unlock the gates and sound the alarm, and while the guards battled his giant friend he'd confront the Troll King himself. By the time Levi got through the quest would be over, all the experience points and bonus items claimed. Drew grinned mischievously. Completing the quest alone would be ten times the insult of any verbal jab.

He'd almost built up the courage to move when voices rang out.

"Hey look, it's Andrew Dennison!"

"You mean Drew the Thief!"

"And Leviathan, the world's biggest pawn!"

"Ha-ha, what a pair of losers!"

Drew swore under his breath. He'd been so focused on his plan that he hadn't noticed two trolls sneaking up on them. It was exactly what he'd been trying to avoid by cycling to the common filter! Now he switched back to it in disgust.

Flabs and Crabs leered at them, two popeyed man-babies with face tattoos and leather jackets. But what caught Drew's eye were their jerry-rigged scooters. In a world without factories, where nearly everything but survival necessities were virtual, working transportation was the gold standard of the economy. That the twins would use scooters to carry themselves around *for entertainment* was a slap in the face of tradition and, frankly, common human decency. They could've met the train and helped transport food across town.

Drew pretended to remove his goggles, like he couldn't believe what he was seeing. "You guys broke your dicks at the same time?"

Crabs scowled. He dropped his scooter and advanced on Drew. "Bet you wish you were invisible now," he said. "Pansy ass pretender."

Drew slid his avatar's short sword out of its scabbard and raised it in the space between them. It was a gentleman's challenge, as the boy could easily brush his empty hand aside and pummel him without reprisal from the software.

Crabs sneered and made to do just that, but Flabs appealed to his brother. "Take him down." After a terse nod Crabs drew a hunting knife, and suddenly Drew wasn't sure it was virtual at all.

"Let's get out of here!" he cried to Leviathan. They turned and ran, not looking back until the twins' vile laughter had faded and they were sure they weren't being followed. They finally stopped, panting, doubled over with their hands on their knees until it was possible to catch a breath.

"That sucked," Drew managed at last.

"I hate those guys," Leviathan muttered. "They've been bullying us since first grade."

"I know."

"Why, just because I'm autistic? I didn't ask to be like this! How do they know anyway? Why doesn't the *algo*rithm protect me?"

"I know why I'm being targeted. *And* not protected," Drew said bitterly.

"Oh crap," said Leviathan. "I'm sorry. I wasn't thinking. Your dad-"

"It doesn't matter."

"I said I'm sorry."

Drew shrugged reactively. It was getting to be a bit much. "I've had enough for today."

As he wandered off, Drew brooded. This was not a typical character trait. He'd never been one to worry about the future. His generation had grown up knowing they would have one and that could certainly have been a part of it, but in a more general sense he just wasn't the type to think outside of the box. His ambitions were all related to leveling up his character. In his view, what had just happened with Flabs and Crabs hadn't only happened because of his father. That may have been the single most important factor, but – like his mom had suggested, he admitted grudgingly – it wouldn't have been possible if he'd had a strong enough avatar to make the twins' efforts too costly to pursue.

He knew the logic was flawed. There would always be someone stronger, always be someone more experienced. He could quest all his life and still get bullied. But what alternative was there?

Drew was so distracted with his dilemma that he nearly stumbled into the twins again.

#

He'd taken the long way around the recessed plateau, a dread sense of anxiety guiding him as much as anything, so when he heard squeaky scooter wheels and dull guffaws Drew slipped between two bushes that could have been garbage cans for all he knew, gripping his short sword in one hand. It was clearly a pointless artifact against real world enemies but it gave him a sense of security.

Flabs and Crabs were flanking someone, a young kid Drew didn't recognize, their scooters blocking any possible exit for their prey. The kid protested feebly while the twins laughed. Then, as Drew watched, Crabs intentionally rolled his scooter over the kid's foot. The kid fell to the ground, crying. The boys laughed and wheeled around for another pass.

Something gave inside of Drew in that moment. All the injustice of the day piled up on top of his childhood trauma and he just couldn't take it anymore. He closed his eyes but his goggle filters transposed the scene onto his eyelids in infrared. He rubbed his face with his hands, then covered the goggles in his palms. A bright redness suffused everything.

Drew dropped his arms and opened his eyes and glared at the world around him with its cheerful brightness and welcoming aura of vigor and health. It was a lie. It was all a lie. He stuck his fingers into the corners of his eyes and pried his goggles loose. With a fatalistic exhalation he removed them.

#

CHAPTER 2

QUEST

The first thing Drew noticed was the light. It was unexpectedly bright even though he'd come directly from the common filter. There must have been some sort of shading mechanism worked into the goggles, he realized, squinting and cupping his palms around his eyes.

The next thing he noticed was the dirt. It was everywhere, from the ground to his clothes to the bushes he'd hidden behind that actually were bushes, though their leaves drooped and were nearly as brown as the ground around them.

The third thing he noticed was Flabs, who was not in fact riding a scooter, and neither was he a popeyed man-baby with face tattoos and a leather jacket. In real life he was a gangly anorexic with a pencil neck strapped to the back of the wheelchair he drove with the one part of his body that was able to move, his right hand.

Crabs was very much as he appeared, but with dirt smears and another sort of brown stain on the seat of his sagging britches.

Drew's eyes finally acclimated enough to be able to remove his hands and take in more than what filtered through his fingers. He was standing at the edge of a clearing with the crumbling remains of a school building behind it. The recessed plateau was an old ball park; a path wound from it and past his hiding place. And standing in the middle of the path, smiling at him oddly, was Mr. Roberts.

Drew's teacher cleared his throat. "I'm sorry to disturb you, Mr. Dennison. Are you okay? You seem... affected."

Dread pulsed through Drew's nervous system. He was still holding his goggles in his fingers. It was too late to put them back on. Any moment now Mr. Roberts would notice he wasn't wearing them. If Flabs or Crabs heard their teacher call him out it was over. He would be branded as his father's son forever.

He cast a desperate look at his teacher. Mr. Roberts had tried to defend him in class. Well, not so much defend his father's actions, but he had tried to shield Drew from the consequences of them. He had no idea if that extended to shielding Drew from the consequences of his own, very similar action, but it seemed to be his last option.

"Please," he started, but immediately stopped. Something was out of place. Mr. Roberts wasn't frowning. He didn't look concerned or suspicious at all. In fact a hint of a smile played at one corner of his lips, and there was a twinkle about his eyes.

His eyes!

Mr. Roberts wasn't wearing goggles either.

#

"Nobody can see that your goggles are out," Mr. Roberts explained as they sauntered along the path. "The rhythms make it work. It's not even that hard; for most of these people you're just a NPC anyway. Your interactions are tuned to stay in character for both parties. Physical changes are easy."

"How did you know?"

Mr. Roberts laughed. "Would you believe it was just good timing?"

Drew thought about it. "No."

"Smart lad. The truth is I've been waiting for the right moment to approach you."

"Approach me? About what?"

"I have a proposition for you. You see, I represent a powerful consortium with a special interest in making contact with a certain group of subversive terrorists."

Drew stopped in his tracks. "You're talking about the Loomies."

Mr. Roberts nodded.

Several seconds passed before Drew continued, his voice incredulous. "You want me to seek out and infiltrate the terrorist organization *you claim* my father was a part of, a decade ago, and introduce you to them? Who the hell do you think you are? And even if I could help you, why would I possibly do it?"

"That is precisely what I am asking," Mr. Roberts replied calmly. "Consider it a quest bequeathed upon you. As to your secondary questions, the answers are one and the same." As Drew watched, Mr. Roberts' face morphed into a face the boy could just recall from a decade ago, though its lines signified the time between had not passed without making its mark. "Now do you understand why I need your help?"

"Dad," Drew gasped. But just as suddenly as his father's face appeared it retracted, the teacher's familiar features again dominating the landscape. "What the hell is going on? How are you doing that without goggles?"

Mr. Roberts replied gravely, "I never said I wasn't wearing goggles."

"But *I'm* not!"

"Mine are a new design. Experimental. They cover my entire face. I can project any face I've seen onto the fabric's matrix."

Drew digested this, the wheels in his mind turning slowly. "My father."

"Yes, Drew. I helped him escape!"

#

"Your father didn't know I helped him," Mr. Roberts clarified. "The consortium I represent arranged to have him transferred to an alternate facility, and on the way... you know the story. Agents hijacked the truck and in the ensuing chaos he got away. His escape was so swift he even left us behind. And so a valuable opportunity was lost. That was two years ago. I have not seen or heard from him since. But I know he's alive."

Drew sat on the sloping edge of the ball park and put his head in his hands. His father was free and had been for two years. Why hadn't he made contact? Were Drew and his mother being watched in case he did? Maybe someone got tired of waiting and sent Mr. Roberts to accelerate things. "How do I know I can trust you? Who do you represent? What is it you plan to do, if you're able to contact the Loomies?" The questions came out in a rush. Drew took his head from his hands and stared at Mr. Roberts, searching for clues even as he wondered if the facial filter was obscuring them.

"Well, I was hoping my story would earn your trust," Mr. Roberts answered. "As for who I represent, I do apologize but we must allow them to remain anonymous for the time being. I can, however, answer your third question. When I am put in contact with the Lumis cult, and I do believe it is more a matter of when than of if, I intend to offer them the full support of my consortium's resources. Which are, I will add, extensive."

#

SIMULUMIS

Drew remained seated on the dirty slope of the old ball park long after Mr. Roberts had concluded his pitch and left. His mind was racing. On the one hand his father was free and it should really have been a no-brainer: go find him! But on the other hand not only did he lack any idea of where to begin such a search, he wasn't certain his father wanted to be found. What was he supposed to say? *Hi dad, remember me? You were arrested when I was five for exposing me to trauma. Hug it out? Oh, and by the way I made a deal with this guy who was pretending to be my teacher in order to find you, but I'm sure he's telling the truth about his intentions.*

The best thing to do would probably be to put his goggles back on and pretend nothing had ever happened. Just flow with the rhythms. Maybe even report Mr. Roberts for soliciting subversion. But how? He didn't have any evidence. He'd taken off his goggles so there wasn't a recording. In fact he would be the one who got in trouble if anyone found out. His teacher had planned it well.

There was another option. He could pretend to do Mr. Roberts' bidding. But instead of introducing the groups he'd warn his father. This would also provide the opportunity to find some answers of his own. He was a Thief after all. It wouldn't be much of a stretch to expand his character into a Spy, a veritable double agent against the powers that be.

How would he start? Reinsert his goggles and join the quotidian. Make a little noise around the edges, ask questions of shady characters until something gave. It sounded like a noir mystery story. Drew fingered the lenses absently. Based on the way he felt in that moment, putting them on would be the equivalent of donning a mask and pretending to be somebody he wasn't – even before any of the spy stuff.

For the first time in his life Drew understood that the world he'd been brought up in was based on lies. Which meant everything he'd identified with, everything he'd taken for granted, was also suspect. The very foundation of his being had come into question. He'd lifted the veil and there was no way to put it back.

Drew was stuck, and he didn't like being stuck. He needed answers. He needed a way forward. On impulse he stood and began walking. He didn't have any goal or destination in mind, he simply needed to move his body. Maybe something would jar loose in his brain.

It was still very bright in the real world. Drew longed suddenly for his elven cloak. He kept to the west side of the old street grid for the shade. Navigation was far more difficult without optimal routes presented in his overlays; what would've been impenetrable thickets or walls, clearly marked as no-man's-land, were now rundown houses wedged between good ones, or burnt husks thereof, and it wasn't always easy to tell the difference. Sinkholes in the crumbling asphalt were common. Sometimes Drew followed other people around these obstacles, confident their navigation systems were functioning properly. Nobody gave him a second look.

And then, entirely without realizing what he'd done, Drew found himself standing outside of Levi's house, hollering at his friend's second-floor bedroom window.

#

The vinyl casement swung open and Leviathan's massive head appeared, careening from side to side to scan the street before settling his gaze on Drew. Goggles shimmering faintly over his eye sockets. He frowned.

"Hail, Drew the Thief. What fair wind hast blown you in my direction?"

"Levi!" Drew hissed. "I need to talk to you. Come down!"

His portly friend's face wrinkled slightly. "The Troll King is dead, I killed him myself. What are you on about?"

"Huh?" Drew stared in confusion. "Just come downstairs!"

Leviathan's eyes hardened. "Your share of the bounty? By what reckoning have you earned it? Are you bewitched?"

Then Drew remembered what Mr. Roberts had said about the internet tuning conversations. Levi must still be in character, and Drew's words were being altered to fit his narrative. So long as he spoke plainly his friend wouldn't hear him.

"Hail, Lord Leviathan!" Drew cried, mustering all the pomp and ritual he could. "Victor of Quest 83, mighty wielder of strength immeasurable. The Troll King is dead! The mission is over! And yet there remains a secret to be found, a hidden treasure within the greater quest. Will you join me to find it, noble comrade?"

"An Easter Egg?" Leviathan blurted, "why didn't you say so? I'll be right there!"

When his friend emerged from the house's front door Drew snuck a peek inside. The hallway was dark and foreboding. Plaster hung off the walls in several places. Somehow the visceral decay reassured him.

Leviathan picked his way down the rotting front steps. Drew had taken them enough times to know what his friend was seeing: a flourishing nursery of potted plants with but a narrow walkway left for access.

Leviathan showed off the booty he'd won by defeating the Troll King. Then they ambled up the street, Drew leading the way. They headed away from the old ball park this time. Drew couldn't tell what his friend was seeing, but in the real world the street grew thinner and the crumbling houses came in greater frequency than the preserved ones. Some were completely covered in ivy. Others had sunk into the bogs that were also appearing with greater frequency, chimneys turned to gravestones, the last testament of their material existence. Eventually the forest canopy stretched above the path altogether and the bright afternoon sun dimmed to flitting rays and intermittent shadows.

For a moment the real world very much resembled a quest module. Drew felt for his sword but found nothing.

All of a sudden Leviathan stopped in his tracks. "Methinks my crafty companion hast attempted to deceive me. Pray tell what is thy game, oh Thief?"

This was it. Drew took a deep breath and began to spin his web.

"A curious thing happened on my way home from the campaign," he said, nonchalantly sticking his hands into the pockets of his synthetic jean pants. "I was accosted by a stranger, only I didn't recognize him as a stranger. I thought I knew exactly who he was. And he told me the most interesting thing." With any luck his words were vague enough that they'd reach Leviathan's ears unimpeded. He looked around dramatically, as if searching for eavesdroppers.

"Who was it?" Leviathan hissed. "What did he say?"

Drew leaned in conspiratorially. Leviathan stooped down to listen, his eyes focusing on a point somewhere in the distance.

"He bequeathed a special quest upon me. One that I am not able to refuse." As he spoke, Drew inched his hands from his pockets and toward Leviathan's face. It had to be uncomfortable for his friend. They were standing so close together. And yet his plan depended on Leviathan's reluctance to make eye contact. "Will you join me? The entire internet hangs in the balance!"

Whether his words were edited or not, enough of the intention got through to produce the result Drew was hoping for. Leviathan jerked alert. He snapped into focus and his head swiveled until his eyes made direct contact with Drew's. "The entire internet? Wait, what are you doing-"

The moment Leviathan's face turned toward his, Drew made his move. His hands were ready. It was an awkward moment as he scrabbled at the lenses, but then he had Leviathan's goggles by the cross piece. He gripped his fingers tightly together and pulled. The goggles popped out with a satisfying ping, like a newly opened jar of blooming algae jam.

#

CHAPTER 3

SUBVERSIVE

Once Drew had calmed his friend down and brought him up to speed on the day's happenings, the gentle giant sat on his haunches and shook his head in amazement. "Mr. Roberts is a subversive," he said. "He groomed you, and now I'm part of it too."

"He didn't though," Drew countered. "Don't you get it? I don't want to find my dad to do Mr. Roberts' bidding. Forget him! I just want to know why he left."

A look of sorrow crossed Leviathan's face. He bit off several replies before heaving a sigh. "Has it occurred to you that Mr. Roberts may be lying?"

"About what, wanting to help my dad take down the internet? If that's his cover story... I mean I can't imagine anything much worse."

"Maybe he wants to stop your dad. Maybe he's never seen him and it's all a trick of his tech. The point is we have no idea. And you know as well as I do that it's unwise to enter into battle without good intelligence."

Drew chewed on the words. He wanted to jump into action, but Leviathan was right. How was he supposed to choose the correct action without a better sense of the quest's landscape?

"So what are we supposed to do, put our goggles back on? Return to school and investigate Mr. Roberts in our spare time? You know we'll just get comfortable and forget any of this happened."

Leviathan bobbed his head in agreement. "That's not what I'm saying at all. In fact, here, let me see yours." He held out a hand. Drew placed his goggles in his friend's palm reflexively. Leviathan set his own next to Drew's and closed his fist around them. Then he lifted his arm and swung it toward the ground, opening his palm at the last second. The goggles shattered.

"What have you done?" Drew cried.

"Now we're committed," said Leviathan with a satisfied grin.

Drew just stared. He was too stunned to reply. Up to this point the entire thing had seemed hypothetical, a thought experiment he was sharing with his friend, nothing they couldn't back out of by putting on their goggles and forgetting it'd ever happened. That was no longer the case. Broken goggles were a rare occurrence, and two pairs breaking at the same time in the same location was bound to set off alarm rhythms. Algorithms, Drew reminded himself.

"We've got to get out of here," he said.

Leviathan clambered to his feet. His satisfied grin had turned sloppy. He was positively beaming. "Come on," he said, loping deeper down the path.

Drew followed closely behind, letting Leviathan clear the cobwebs. They walked for an hour without seeing any signs of civilization, not a single person or house or street. It was like the forest had swallowed the city up, every trace of humanity erased.

Twice they'd seen eyes in the depths of the trees, and once an animal crossed their path, but so far nothing had challenged them beyond the terrain. Eventually they'd need shelter, and water, and if this charade didn't bring itself to a conclusion soon, food as well.

"Where are we going?" Drew said at last. He stopped, panting. They'd been walking beside a slough, one of the foul bogs whose fingers had begun to inundate the city, the ancient swamp rising up to reclaim its birthright. But this was a different level altogether. The slough receded into blackness as far as they could see, the forest blocking any sun or sense of direction. "Are you trying to get us lost?"

Leviathan placed a hand on his shoulder. "Don't be alarmed, little buddy, but we're on a real adventure now. Getting lost is the easy part."

With a deep sense of fatalism Drew provided the requisite line. "What's the hard part?"

Leviathan directed a stubby arm toward the slough. "Finding our way through."

#

Drew took a careful step into the muck, resisting the urge to let out a sigh. This was the way forward. It was obvious as soon as Leviathan explained it to him. That didn't mean he had to like it.

They were trying to hide from a computer network whose eyes and ears quite literally belonged to the people using its algorithms. To escape its sight, then, they had to go where none of its users ever went.

Of course there were the bumblebee drones to consider, and Mr. Roberts' consortium, who would likely send agents after them; but no plan was perfect, and honestly he was just glad to have someone sharing the experience.

Like most people in his generation, Drew had been raised to believe two things: that the internet was the greatest of mankind's inventions to ever grace the face of the earth, and that without it humanity would descend into a dark age so terrible it would never recover. The brutality of the Great Interruption still shaded their existence, and it was hard to dispute the facts. Six billion people had died. Three quarters of the world population just gone, victims of pettiness and greed. No wonder his grandparents' generation had accepted the technological armistice. It ensured mutual survival, and did so without anybody having to admit they were wrong.

Drew had never questioned the system. There was no reason to. You followed the rules and leveled up your character and the rhythms took care of you. He'd never fought a boss he didn't have an outsider's chance to defeat. Sure, the twins could gang up on him, but that didn't gain them experience points and they usually bored of it pretty quick, so it wasn't really all that bad.

The point was that Drew, and everyone he knew, were all operating under the assumption that their thoughts, moves, and actions were being guided by the invisible hand of a benevolent program with an overarching plan to care for their well-being. But now, for the first time in his adult life, Drew was operating without that safety net.

#

They made camp on the far side of the mother slough. At least that's what Drew called it. By the time they reached solid ground the sun must have set, for the wan light had dimmed nearly to blackness. Neither boy carried torch nor flame, or any survival equipment whatsoever. Their shelter consisted of wallowing into a shallow section of the slough that was sheltered by an embankment.

"What do you think is happening in town?" Drew asked idly.

Leviathan let out a guffaw, the mud around his body squelching in chorus. "My parents are probably freaking out."

"My mom too."

Leviathan sat up abruptly. "What if your dad's really close? What if he's, like, right here in the slough with us?"

"What? Why?" Drew resisted the urge to hope, but his heart leapt in his chest nonetheless. "That sounds way too coincidental."

"It all depends on Roberts," Leviathan said, and whether he dropped the Mr. on purpose or not Drew couldn't tell, but from that point forward that was what they called him. "Why did he approach you now? Why not two years ago, when he claims your father escaped? It doesn't make sense unless he knows exactly where your father is. I think he can't get to him on his own. But he thinks you can." He laid back down in the bog, the mud covering barely half his body. He spooned it over himself absently.

Drew tried to imagine his father living in the slough with a group of subversive terrorists, plotting the downfall of the internet, the digital lifeline of civilization, the only thing separating humanity from the parade of animals marching toward extinction or already there. He tried to imagine what traumatic experience could have led him down such a path. He nestled deeper into the mud until only his face peeked out. Eventually he slept.

#

SIMULUMIS

The orc horde attacked in the darkest hour of the night.

Drew woke to a flaming arrow quivering in the ground beside him. He fought the urge to bolt upright. Leviathan was snoring fitfully. A thick mist rose off the bog.

Then Drew saw the orcs. There were six of them, each uglier than the last. Their faces seemed simultaneously shrunken and swollen, with crinkled bodies more suitable for contortion than conveyance, their slender appendages a devil's compromise between fingers and tentacles. Each orc carried weapons of some kind. The smallest appeared to be weighed down by a burden, which he dropped to the ground next to Drew's supine body.

"Eh," the little orc squeaked, "you missed the biggest target in the forest!"

"Tell me something I don't know," grumbled an orc holding a crossbow. It gripped the blazing arrow and jerked it from the ground.

Drew realized the orcs couldn't see him. So long as he kept quiet he'd be safe. Defeating them in battle was another story. He was a Thief, not a Warrior. That was Leviathan's job.

Leviathan! While he dithered his friend was in mortal danger. The orcs had closed in on the sleeping giant, their weapons drawn and poised. One appeared to be casting a spell. Drew sat upright and opened his mouth to shout, but was struck silent as his eyes fell on the discarded bundle lying on the ground beside him.

His classmate Sera Hector was staring up at him. She was bound from head to toe in rough, chafing ropes and her mouth was gagged with a piece of cloth, but she could move her head. It was shaking slowly from side to side.

Drew gathered his wits and inched toward the bound maiden. When he was close enough he reached out to untie her bonds, being careful to keep out of the light of the orcs' torches. Sera pulled the gag from around her neck. She watched Drew with careful eyes. Her head tilted toward the bog, a silent invitation.

Drew's eyes darted to his friend, who was now snoring even louder. He was surely under a spell, but what was the orcs' plan? He looked to his new companion in query.

She leaned toward him and put her mouth to his ear. "They won't sacrifice him until sunrise on the morrow. We can return with a plan, but if it pleases you let us flee this ambuscade ere our window of opportunity closes!"

Drew did as she said and they slipped out of camp without being noticed. He didn't ask questions, even after they'd left the orcs far behind. It wasn't an abundance of caution. He simply didn't believe anything that was happening was real. How could it be? He wasn't wearing goggles. This was clearly a dream.

It was hardly a surprise, then, when he tripped over a root and the ground rushed up to greet him.

#

Drew groaned as consciousness returned. He'd slept poorly, and not without nightmares. Maybe that was to be expected. He'd never gone camping before, and spending the night in a mud bog barely qualified anyway. His mouth was parched. He tried to draw up saliva to wet his lips but just made it worse. He experimented with opening his eyes and immediately regretted it.

"What were we thinking?" he said, vaguely addressing Leviathan. "We can't keep doing this. We have to go home and face the consequences. If we can even find our way back."

"Fair knight, are you hale?" said a voice.

Drew groaned again. He cracked an eye open, this time focusing in the direction of the voice. It was definitely not Leviathan. But who else-

He sat up abruptly, causing his head to spin. It took all his concentration to keep from collapsing. After an intermittent time the feeling passed, blood returned to his head, and he was able to open his eyes completely. "Sera. You're really here."

The object of his youthful affections favored him with a half-smile. She wore a nondescript synthetic jumpsuit much like his clothes, though hers hadn't seen the inside of a bog with the same intimacy. She held herself like royalty.

"Milord knows my name."

"Sera, it's me! Drew Dennison. From school!" He broke off at her puzzlement. Had she never noticed him? He supposed it was possible. He felt his cheeks growing red. Apparently his secret affections were not mutual.

"You poor thing," she was saying, "you're not making sense. You must still be feeling the effects of your injury. Were we in Camelot I could hasten you to the medic, but we aren't, and your friend lacks the time for us to travel to and fro. We must return at once to free him or I fear we shall arrive too late."

Oh, right. His words and appearance were being edited. She literally couldn't see him for who he was. Drew briefly considered an assault on her goggles, but one look at his companion dissuaded him of the notion. She was every bit the Warrior that Leviathan was, minus the goofy awkwardness. He struggled to his feet, hyper-aware of the proximity of her body as she steadied him until he could stand on his own.

"Lead on, Xena," he said, and was rewarded with a piercing glare.

He fell in step behind her, content to watch the stride of her legs, the sway of her hips, and, okay, the way her butt moved as she navigated the forest. He began to imagine a situation in which they were forced to camp together for days and nights, even weeks, just the two of them, the quest stringing out so long that they'd forget the world they came from.

When they came to the bog Sera called for a halt, which was to say she stopped walking and got down on her knees. Drew followed suit, and the two of them proceeded to rub mud into their hair.

They practically swam through the bog this time, and whether it proved better camouflage in the real world or on the internet, it allowed them to sneak up on the orcs and steal their weapons before they even knew they were being attacked. The ambushed turned ambushers whooped and hollered as they raided the orcs' camp, dousing lights and delivering blows until the demon spawn scuttled away into the night.

Sera chanted a counter spell and slapped Leviathan's face. "Wake up, big boy. Our esteemed foes are undoubtedly fetching reinforcements."

Leviathan sat up, shaking his head groggily. He reached out and grabbed Sera with both hands, lifting her off the ground. "Drew? Who the hell is this dame?"

"Put me down, sleeping beauty!" Sera insisted. "I saved you!"

"Ew!" Leviathan dropped her hastily. He wiped the back of his other hand across his mouth. "You *kissed* me?"

"You wish, you overgrown cherub!" Sera glared at Drew, adjusting her muddy clothes righteously. "If your noble companion here hadn't avowed me your lifelong service I'd have left you to the orc horde."

Leviathan turned to stare at Drew. "You did what?"

#

Drew gazed at his companions across the flames, their three bodies making an equilateral triangle with the fire in the center, a pyramid to light their night. Sera had taken an ember from the orcs' fire when they'd abandoned camp, and now – a good two hours and at least a mile away – she'd rekindled it into a blazing fire for them to dry around as the night stretched on.

Drew had never managed to keep more than one friend at a time. On some level he knew this was a character flaw, not something based off his thief's attributes but an actual real life character flaw that he, Andrew Dennison, had drawn from the human gene pool when he'd entered the world. And so, as one did with the traits that came with an avatar's identity, he'd played to his strengths. He'd always made sure he had one *good* friend.

But now that strategy was proving to be flawed, or at least to have a very low ceiling.

He cleared his throat. "I think we should work together."

Leviathan and Sera immediately raised their voices in protest.

Drew waved at them with an authority he wasn't feeling. "Look, I know we come from different places. Different backgrounds, different filters." He directed his stare at Leviathan. "But if we speak clearly and with pure intention, I think we can help each other."

"I'm picking up what you're putting down," Leviathan said, the hint of a grin playing across his lips.

"You said we needed information. You also said nobody would be out here. Well, seeing that somebody is out here maybe this is our best chance to get that information. Who are those guys, and what were they doing? Why were their bodies so misshapen? Do they have experimental tech too?"

Leviathan had adjusted his posture to face Sera. He was muttering under his breath. "I'll hold her down. You take her goggles off."

"Wait, what?" Drew shook his head. "That's not what I meant!"

Leviathan frowned. "How can she help us when she can't even hear our words?" He flapped a hand in Sera's general direction. "Here birdie! See? She doesn't have a clue!"

Suddenly Sera's sword arm shot out and twisted Leviathan's wrist. The giant rolled onto the ground, squealing in surprise. "I know not what you two speak of, for your words are muddied by fatigue," Sera said, "but I can recognize disrespect when I see it. Were you a more worthy lad I would make an example of you!" She let go of his arm disdainfully. It fell to the ground. "And now," she announced, "I see the light of dawn is upon us. I must depart this swamp and seek out the palace of Camelot. If you… gentlemen can postpone your quest to act as my couriers for but a day I can promise you a noble welcome upon arrival."

Leviathan picked himself off the ground gingerly. "Did you say Camelot?"

#

"I can't believe we're going to Camelot," Leviathan grinned over his shoulder, pausing in his work of clearing a path through the forest.

A short second behind him, Drew stepped over a fallen limb. "It won't be Camelot," he said, the tone of his voice making it clear he'd said it before.

Sera's stolen orc sword swished through the underbrush behind him. "I should lead," she remarked with a similar intonation.

It was nearing the end of the day and they still hadn't reached the edge of the forest. They'd barely eaten anything since the debacle started and had only sipped water from the lone stream they'd crossed, Sera's warning of the real life danger of dysentery taken to heart. They hadn't taken an ember from the previous night's fire.

Then the forest ended. Like, abruptly. One moment they were crashing through trees and the next Leviathan was taking a pratfall into open water. Sera and Drew laughed as the giant struggled to his feet. A piece of algae hung from his hair.

"Look!" said Drew. He was squinting at the opposite shore. Little but outlines could be seen in the waning light, yet even so the structure was too large to miss. It stretched ten times higher than it was wide. There were three peaks, each a pinnacle atop a tower, the one in the middle standing tallest.

"Camelot," Leviathan whispered.

This time Drew didn't contradict him.

"Let us pitch camp," said Sera. "We shall cross in the morning."

#

They spooned at the edge of the forest, first Drew and then Sera and finally Leviathan's bulk as a windbreaker. The night was fortunately mild, though Drew would not have noticed arctic conditions so enraptured was he with the feeling of his body pressed against Sera's. They fell to talking in quiet whispers, and Drew studiously pretended he didn't know anything about her personal life already. She was a year older than he; had two siblings, a sister who bugged the daylights out of her and a brother she adored; she thought quests were juvenile but the best way to score easy coin; and, most importantly, she did not have a special someone in her life at the moment. That detail made Drew exhale in a way he hoped no one noticed.

"What of thyself?" Sera asked, patting Drew's leg. "What are you most passionate about, once your quest is said and done?"

"The next quest!" said Leviathan, laughing.

Drew scowled. Maybe it was true, but he didn't have to point it out. Not when she'd clearly said she thought quests were juvenile. "Probably check on my mom," he mumbled. "Sleep in my own bed. I don't know."

"A man of the people. My father would approve."

"And with that, I'm going to sleep," Leviathan announced. Soon he could be heard snoring halfway across the river.

Drew lay next to Sera for an indeterminate length of time. The sky had opened up and for the first time since they'd entered the forest they could see stars. He'd never felt more content than in that moment, his arm laying across her midriff, staring into the heavens, the pulse of the river vibrating below them.

Then the moon came out.

Common sense says that stars grow dimmer in the light of the moon, but it did not feel that way. Where one minute they'd been an isolated speck floating below an infinite universe, the next Drew was suddenly very aware of their surroundings, for the moon lit up everything, from the sky to the river to the gigantic castle that stood but a kilometer away. It might have been made of mirrors, for stars shone across its turrets and walls.

Drew sat up on an impulse.

Beside him, Sera stirred. "What ails you, comrade?"

He struggled for words. "Have you ever done something you knew was wrong, like you'd been told your entire life not to do, and it turned out to be the most exciting thing you'd ever experienced?"

Sera rolled onto her back to look up at him. "Ay, the forbidden is often the most enticing."

"Is that all this is?" Drew gestured at the night. "A forbidden fantasy?"

Sera didn't answer. A bat swooped over them and darted away, squeaking.

"What if I wake up tomorrow and none of this happened?"

Now she sat up and faced him, their profiles stretching shadows across the moonlight.

"What would you most regret not doing?"

Drew blushed and looked away, hoping the shadows would conceal his embarrassment. Was she saying what it sounded like she was saying? There was a certain storybook quality to it: he'd saved the princess and now she was offering him a reward. Though in truth he'd done little more than untie her bonds and she'd done the rest, including saving Leviathan, who most definitely was not serving up kisses of gratitude.

If he was misreading the situation, and if Sera remembered it, goggles or no goggles, there was no doubt it would become the thing he most regretting *doing*.

Besides, he'd never kissed anyone before.

"What happened out there," he asked instead, "how'd the orcs catch you?"

The moment passed. Sera nestled back onto the ground. "A spell was cast upon me," she answered at length. "I could neither see nor hear my foes. It was an uncommon piece of magic, Lord Dennison, for I could detect no trace of its caster."

"You're a magic user?"

"I make use of the tools in my arsenal, yes."

"Of course," Drew hastened to agree. "I didn't mean anything."

"It is not a crutch, if you are insinuating such a thing. I have defeated two hundred bosses without magic."

"Two hundred?" Drew gasped. "We're only on quest eighty-three!"

"Quests are basic," Sera said, her voice betraying a loss of interest. "I simply kill everything in my way. Now lie down and warm my backside, that we may wake in the morning at all."

#

The next morning Leviathan didn't say anything, but something had changed. He didn't look either of them in the eyes, and at the first polite opportunity took his leave to scout out the best way for them to cross the river.

Sera used her sword to sharpen a stick for herself and another for Drew; they took them to the river's edge and made a futile attempt to spear fish. After a while Leviathan returned to mumble, eyes downcast, that there were no thin stretches to the river but a ways downstream an island split it in two. It sounded like their best bet so Drew and Sera fell in line behind the gloomy giant. They walked until the sun was directly overhead and Drew was fairly panting.

"There," Leviathan said.

Drew followed the giant's gaze and sucked in his breath. An island did indeed split the river in half, but the water moved swiftly on either side. Even if they'd had a boat it would have been treacherous to cross. Was his friend messing with them?

Sera echoed his thoughts. "My good Lord is surely jesting?"

"What?" Leviathan grumbled. "This is totally doable."

"Perhaps for you, Hercules!" She spoke so vehemently that both Drew and Leviathan flinched in surprise. "Oh, you had not considered whether the fair lady could swim?" She folded her arms across her chest and turned her back on them.

Leviathan shot Drew an expectant look. He awkwardly put an arm around Sera's shoulder. "It's okay. We'll find another way."

"I'm sorry," Leviathan added, his body language stiff. "I didn't know. I wasn't thinking."

"Then pray tell what's been nagging you all day?" Sera turned to face him, subtly easing Drew's arm off her shoulder in the process. "Wherefore art thou being such a dick?"

"Why do you think?" Leviathan yelled. "I've gone from sidekick to third wheel!"

Drew didn't move. Neither did Sera. They just stared at him, their jaws open, like he'd suddenly admitted to masterminding the whole fiasco, that old trope of the best friend as the villain come to life.

"My Lord Leviathan," Sera began, speaking in the most formal manner she had since they'd crossed paths, "There is nothing between your friend the thief and myself to be envious of, as I am not the type of person to fall for the first responder that happens along. I assure you our paths will diverge soon upon arrival at our destination."

"Your destination, you mean."

"Is that truly what is eating you?"

Leviathan scowled and turned to Drew, who had been watching the exchange in a mortified stupor. This was why he could only keep one friend at a time. Eventually they'd force him to take sides and he'd lose one of his friends, or both if he wasn't careful.

But instead of arguing, Leviathan started laughing. "You should see yourself!" he hooted. "You're drooling!"

Drew wiped at his jaw, which set Sera off. Then they were all laughing hysterically, and whether any of them *didn't* drool over the next few minutes was as unlikely as the reason they were laughing in the first place.

#

It was two days before they attempted the crossing. Two languid days of working and joking with Sera and Leviathan, who'd gotten over their tiff and grown closer for it. They'd built a raft from driftwood and roughly braided cedar bark, and if it didn't last beyond the journey hopefully it would at least last *through* it. As a precaution he'd done his best to teach Sera to swim, though the lessons had as often as not devolved into splashing contests.

At times Leviathan would set off by himself to look for nuts and berries and return in a somber mood. After one such occasion Sera and Drew cornered him.

"We don't want you to feel like a third wheel," Drew explained, "but it's hard when you go off by yourself so much of the time."

"It's just the way I am," Leviathan mumbled. "Don't worry about it."

"If 'tis me, I can leave," Sera said quietly, raising a hand before Drew could protest.

Leviathan shook his head, keeping his eyes on the ground. "It's a lot, you know, just being in this body. Though I guess you don't know. How could you? I have to be aware of my own parts at all times so I don't bump into things and knock into people and annoy everyone around me." As he spoke Leviathan's voice gained courage, and momentum, like the words had been bottled up inside him because nobody had given him the time and space in which to speak them, and now they were pouring forth with a power of their own. "I don't know how it is for everyone else, but when the people around you – even the algorithms – are constantly telling you that you're a burden, you come to believe them. So if I've developed a habit of going off by myself can you really blame me?

"And no, I'm not jealous of you guys. Even if there was something between you, I'd be happy for you while also being a little bit sad that that kind of relationship is probably going to be something I never experience. The sexual part anyway. Do I want romantic love, to sail off into a metaphorical sunset? Sure. But how am I supposed to find another person that can't stand physical contact?"

They caught sight of people across the river. One had waved to them in a very specific pattern, but the group was divided on the meaning of the gesture. Sera thought it was a warning against crossing. Leviathan read it as an invitation, and Drew simply couldn't tell. He didn't much care, either. These were the best days of his life. He didn't want their journey to ever end.

But on the morning of the third day they packed their meager belongings onto the makeshift raft and pushed off from the southern shore. Sera stood awkwardly at the stern using a branch as a guide pole. Drew lay sprawled on the deck, simultaneously acting as a counterweight and a human clamp for the deck's shifting timbers. The raft was not built well. Its main beam, the one Sera was balanced on and which currently seemed to be jammed halfway up Drew's ass, was tied to Leviathan with a cedar bark rope. At first he'd pulled them but now he trailed behind, doling out the line more quickly than seemed appropriate.

"I think something's wrong," Sera said in just that moment.

"We're going too fast!" Drew called out.

"It's too deep for him to follow." Sera said, glancing backwards.

"What do we do?" Drew cried. It occurred to him that, for someone who couldn't swim, she was much calmer than he was.

"I don't know if-"

There was a jerk, and Sera fell to her knees. Drew heard Leviathan shout. The raft was fighting the current, bobbing in the water.

"This is the end of the line!" Drew yelled maniacally.

Sera shot him a look that held a promise of a smack to his head, once they got out of this. "It's too fast!" She waved at the giant. "Pull us back!"

Leviathan heaved at the rope, and the raft fell apart.

#

CHAPTER 4

THE ISLAND

Drew became conscious. He'd not been aware that he wasn't conscious, which made him wonder what had caused him to not be conscious, which brought up the question of where he was and just what was going on in the first place. It all rather gave him a headache. If he lay there and moaned maybe his mom would bring him treats and let him skip out on school for the day.

"Easy, mister. You've had a bad accident."

It wasn't his mother's voice. Despair flowed over him. Drew knew he was going to have to open his eyes, but that would make it real, all of it, and he wasn't ready to face what that meant. Not yet.

"It's lucky you're so small," the voice continued. "I was just able to pull you out. Any bigger and you would've drowned, like your friend."

Drew bolted upright. He was lying on a crude cot under a rough lean to. His left arm was bandaged and there was a gash running down his cheek. A girl of maybe ten stood over him, hair poking out in tiny dreadlocks, sporting a crooked grin like a feral cat. No trace of goggles occluded her eyesight.

Drew threw up in her face.

#

Later, because he felt bad but also because he had no choice, he talked to the girl, whose name he learned was – quite appropriately – Gabby.

"People used to crash here all the time," Gabby informed him, "but nobody tries anymore. Why bother, when there's a bridge a day's walk upriver?"

"We didn't know," Drew said lamely.

The girl shook her head in disbelief. "Questers."

"You're not part of the rhythm," Drew said. The cogs in his mind began turning, however slowly. "Are you with Lumis?"

"I don't know what that means."

"Sorry. What's the name of this land? Kingdom? Domain?"

She shrugged. "I live on the island."

"Sure, but what about before?"

She stared at him and giggled. "You must've swallowed too much water, mister."

#

Memories flooded him when he slept. He would jerk awake, gripping Gabby's cot convulsively, convinced the raft was falling apart again, his fingers white from the effort. He sweated so bad his earnest host had to rinse his sheets each day. Where she slept he didn't know, and suspected she preferred it that way.

He woke up screaming.

Gabby wasn't there. Drew sat up and ran his good hand through his hair. How long had he been wallowing in pity? He had a vague memory of learning that grief came in stages, but he didn't have a clue as to what the stages were or where he might be on their continuum. If he'd been online he would've been able to look it up without thinking.

Having nothing else to do, Drew paced the perimeter of the lean to, touching the random pieces of flotsam and jetsam Gabby had collected. A shiny stone caught his eye. He took to carrying it with him, and at intervals would tap it against other rocks. One day a spark flew off the point of impact. Drew hollered in excitement.

He spent the rest of the day outside. The island was bigger than he remembered, or maybe he'd never seen more than the tip of it in the first place. In any case the hut was in a small clearing between two grassy dunes. Behind it the land rose above the dunes and was just as forested as the mainland. A thin trail circled the dense interior.

He joined the path and began walking.

SIMULUMIS

That night, when Gabby arrived with a handful of berries for dinner, Drew was waiting. He'd gathered kindling and firewood and built a tipi at the point of the island, where it would be visible from both shores of the mainland. He'd wadded duff into a cradle for the sparks to land in.

Drew gripped the shiny stone in his good hand and put the rock in his other one. He swung at it clumsily. Gabby giggled. He tried again, then switched them. This time a few tired sparks made it halfway to the duff bed. Gabby gasped in surprise. He grinned, buoyed by her enthusiasm, and made several hard swings. Sparks flew at the duff and stuck. He dropped his tools and picked up the glowing pile and blew on it, vaguely hearing Gabby whoop in delight. A flame burst into being. He gave it another blow and then stuck the whole kit and caboodle under the tipi. Within minutes it was blazing.

"You're a wizard!" yelled Gabby.

"No, I'm lost," said Drew, "and I have no idea what to do next."

#

Drew lit a fire each night for the next three nights. He spent the days gathering wood and helping Gabby collect berries. He'd tried to get more information from her but she just kept repeating *I live on the island* until he gave up in frustration, at which point she started crying, so he made sure not to ask again.

She was a strange girl. He couldn't take anything about her for granted, as he learned the day he built his last fire. He didn't know it was going to be his last fire, but even so something must have felt different, because that night he opened up and told her about Sera. He told her everything, from the moment he'd spotted her in first grade to rescuing her from the orc horde to the last moment he'd seen her, when the raft log had rolled and they'd been swept under the water. He told her how he'd realized he didn't want to go home, only to lose her within days. And now he was lost. He might as well go home and face the consequences.

Gabby sat by the fire and listened to every word without interrupting once, a personal record. Then she sighed and pointed at the fire. "That's why you've been lighting these. But are you trying to get rescued or imprisoned?"

"I just want it to be over," Drew said lamely. "It doesn't matter. Sera's dead."

"You don't know that for sure."

Drew stared at the girl. Somehow, without his noticing or it seeming at all strange, she had grown into a wizened old lady. "But she drowned. You said so yourself!"

"Maybe she did and maybe she didn't."

"Wait." Drew rubbed his temples. "What are you saying?"

"Much of your story does not add up, Drew Dennison. The subversive teacher. The magic goggles. The quest only you can complete because of your familial ties. Real life orcs, and a stereotypical warrior princess. You should consider the possibility that you do not have a complete understanding of the rules and rhythms that govern the disparate planes of reality you seem to be flitting between."

Drew forced himself to think as hard as he could. "If someone has a technology so advanced it's like magic, there's no saying what is and isn't real."

"Bravo," said Gabby, slow clapping and rising to her feet. "My work here is done."

"Your work-"

She giggled, an adolescent mannerism that no longer seemed to suit her. "What did you think NPCs were, freeloaders? We have jobs too!"

"Thanks," Drew said.

"Don't worry about it!" She stepped backwards, fading into the night. "Do yourself a favor though and take the bridge next time. Oh, and tell Leviathan he should visit. I live on the island."

"Levi's here?" Drew gasped. "How do I find him?"

Gabby was barely visible, her voice a whisper in the wind. "The rescue boat's already landed."

#

CHAPTER 5
RESURRECTION

The first thing Leviathan did when Drew told him what Gabby said was roll his eyes. "Clarke's Third Law," he said. "Lame."

"I'm not even going to pretend I know what that means."

They sat on the northern side of the river, Leviathan's legs dangling into the swiftly flowing water, Gabby's island looming in the distance. Drew kept away from the edge. A picnic blanket was laid out between them sporting a bread board with homemade algae cakes and fresh picked berries, a gift from his rescuers. The blanket's edges were pressed into the grass with the weight of two swords.

Drew sampled the cakes hesitantly, their taste new without the goggles' sensory intervention. He passed on the berries.

"Once upon a time there was an elderly, distinguished scientist," Leviathan began, speaking around mouthfuls of cakes, "who liked to test the limits of the possible. Since the society he lived in was a chaotic mess of competition and corruption and it was hard to actually accomplish anything, these experiments tended to take the form of stories. Every once in a while he'd come up with an idea that would change the world. He invented the satellite system our internet makes use of, for example. And one of his laws, which was really just a unique way of looking at things, stated that sufficiently advanced technology would resemble, or be indistinguishable from, magic."

"It explains the orcs," Drew said hesitantly.

"It explains nothing!" Leviathan exploded. "It's an ad hoc theory! All it does is in effect say we don't have any idea what's going on. How is that helpful?" Leviathan threw a berry into his mouth and lapsed into silence.

Drew took advantage of the pause in the conversation to work through the consequences of his friend's words. "But really that's what Gabby was saying too. I should consider the possibility that I don't have a complete understanding of the rules and rhythms that govern disparate planes of reality. And she said it in direct reference to my comment about Sera having drowned."

"Disparate planes of reality," Leviathan echoed. His eyes glazed over. He began whispering it to himself quietly. "Disparate planes of reality."

Drew knew Leviathan well enough to give him time to process. He contented himself throwing berries into the river and gnawing on a cake. A thought was forming in the back of his mind. He couldn't put it into words, but there was a reassuring feeling about it. Like he'd just solved a puzzle he'd been working on for a long time.

Finally Leviathan gave a start and came to with a sigh. "I'm stumped. I don't know what she meant. There's the real world and the internet, and I'm pretty sure I understand the internet's rules and rhythms better, but if I know one thing about this place," he gestured at random, "it's that there's no such thing as a do over. If you die here that's it."

In that moment Drew took the biggest leap of logic he'd ever taken in his life. "What if this isn't her real world?"

Leviathan dropped his algae cake.

#

"Walk me through it again," said the striding giant.

Drew sucked in his breath. They'd bypassed Camelot and crossed the bridge and were now retracing their steps through the forest to return to the mother slough. "What do we know for a fact?" he asked, and began ticking point off on his fingers. "My father was a Loomie. He got arrested for taking off my goggles. Then, the very first time I removed them on my own, Mr. Roberts just happened to be standing right there – also without goggles. As a result of that encounter I enlisted you to join me on this quest and we fled into the slough, where we were attacked by a horde of orcs, which – I remind you – only exist in our imaginations and on the internet."

"Then we met Sera," Leviathan picked up the thread, "who was very definitely still online. And yet we were able to converse with her well enough. Until your raft capsized and you got stranded on that island with the girl, Gabby-"

"She was a sibyl," Drew said. "An oracle."

"That sibyl, Gabby," Leviathan amended, "who got offended when Don Juan here suggested she was a freeloading NPC. And that brings us up to the present moment, but it doesn't explain the mind-bending conclusion you've come to."

"It goes back to Roberts," Drew said. "I think you were right. There's not any reason for him to contact me unless I could reach my father easily. So that's part of it. But why would he divulge the existence of a piece of future tech to a kid like me? He could just as easily have shown me a picture of my dad's face on a vidscreen or something."

"He wanted you to know about it."

"Or believe it existed, anyway. Remember he didn't actually show me the tech."

Leviathan slowed down as he thought about it. "Hiding a bigger lie behind a small one? Or Loomie bait?"

Drew shrugged. "It wouldn't make sense for the Loomies to want the tech, that goes against their mission statement. They might want to know about it in order to destroy it."

"We need to know who Roberts represents. Whose side he's on."

"There's one more thing," said Drew, picking up the pace. "How did the orcs know we were there?"

"You think this was arranged."

"It's too neat. Too much like a normal quest. I think we're being set up."

"By whom?"

But no matter how hard he thought about it, Drew couldn't come up with an answer to that question.

\#

They walked for the rest of the afternoon and all of the next day, retracing their steps through the forest. Around midday on the second day they reached their first campground beside the bog that Drew had named the mother slough.

"And now we wait," said Leviathan, settling down in the exact spot in which he'd been captured several days ago. Drew nodded tersely, too wound up to talk. He gathered firewood and set to work with the flint and steel he'd absconded from Gabby's island. His arm had healed enough to take off the sling. It was still sore, but so long as he didn't stress it he was able to function more or less normally again. He set half a dozen sword-length branches aside, their tips sharp and dripping with pitch.

\#

The orc horde attacked in the darkest hour of the night. This time the boys were ready. Leviathan bashed two with his fists. Hidden by the bog, Drew thrust a stick in the fire and flung the burning branch at the horde. It must've looked daunting, the spear rising from the fire and flying at them, for the orcs shrieked as they dodged the flaming branch. This gave Leviathan time to wind up another blow.

The burdened orc turned and fled. Not waiting to see what happened to the rest of them, Drew drew his sword and gave chase. The forest was dark and he would've been better off with a fire branch, but there was no time to go back and swap weapons. The orc, weighed down as it was, moved quickly through the trees. Drew followed as much by sound as sight until the orc's footfalls abruptly stopped and he found himself alone in the darkness.

He stood as still as he possibly could and listened, his ears straining to make sense of the silence. His breath and the pounding of his heart overrode everything for a while, until he learned to filter them out and listen to the night.

Something was out there. He was being stalked as much as he was the stalker. He gripped his sword tightly. This was it! This was the role he was supposed to fill. And if he did it properly-

The orc glided out of the darkness and swiped at his injured side. Drew barely dodged the attack, remembering at the last instant to thrust with his sword. He was rewarded with an evil shriek, then maniacal laughter.

It came at him again. Drew parried and thrust.

And again.

And again.

On its fifth attack Drew stuck out his foot as he dodged. The orc tripped and fell to the ground. Drew was on it in an instant, the tip of his sword pricking the back of the vile creature's neck. He hovered over it. All it would take was to press his weight into the sword.

Of a sudden a picture of Flabs and Crabs flew into Drew's mind, how they'd cornered the kid in the park that day and knocked him to the ground. But it wasn't popeyed man-babies he saw doing the bullying: it was pathetic, unhappy kids, one in a wheelchair and the other with shit stains on the seat of his pants.

Drew eased the pressure off his sword and stepped away from the orc. His eyes must've acclimated to the darkness because he could just see his misshapen foe clamber to its feet and brush itself off.

"Thought you were going to do me for real there," the orc said ruefully. "Appreciate the mercy, guvnor."

"Don't make me regret it." Drew began thrashing through the bushes, looking for the missing bundle. Sera had managed to push herself into a sitting position and was in the process of gnawing through her gag.

"Thank you kindly, stranger," she said, once he'd pulled what was left of it out of her mouth. "Five more minutes and I've have chewed myself free."

Drew flinched at her words. "You don't remember me."

She appeared to study his features in the gloomy darkness. "Have we met?"

With a sinking sense of déjà vu, Drew responded, "it's Drew Dennison. From school."

The warrior princess shook her head faintly. Drew heaved a sigh and began sawing at her bonds with the business edge of his sword. She was nearly free when a twig snapped. They froze. Drew gripped the hilt and prepared to defend them.

"I say, guvnor," the defeated orc called from the darkness, "did you say your name was Drew Dennison?"

#

"I don't understand," said Sera, scowling into the fire. "Why would you say I'm dead?"

They'd returned to their campsite, captive orc in tow. Apparently Leviathan had had a similar idea because the other five orcs were slumped around the fire, nursing their various wounds. The giant covered them with his sword drawn and at the ready.

"That's not what I meant," Drew said, regretting his decision to explain things on his own. It had all made sense in his head, but even he was having a hard time believing the words that were coming out of his mouth. "You have to think of it symbolically."

"What part?" Sera snapped back. "If these things happened why can I not recall them?"

Drew appealed to his friend with a forlorn glance.

"What if we're all bits and bytes," the giant said, "artificial NPCs in each other's realities. In Drew's story he met you and lost you. Now it used to be that that would be that. But somehow the rules have changed, and here we are."

"That's impossible."

"Is it? I've been doing a lot of thinking, and here's what I've come up with. During the Great Interruption, when the new internet was being built, humanity was at the peak of its technological prowess. Processing power was nearly infinite. Now the story we're told is that they created a coherent system designed to last indefinitely into the future. But why would they put all their eggs in one basket?"

The captive orcs seemed to be watching Leviathan with special interest.

"Why not create billions of realities? A sim for everyone. That way if something glitches it can be cordoned off from the collective, and in the meantime the overlap enriches everyone's experience."

"Whose reality is this then?" Sera scowled. "It does feel real to me."

"We have to consider the possibility that our moves are being guided toward a goal we have no conception of," Leviathan pressed. "We aren't heroes in this world. We're pawns."

"But whose world?" Sera insisted. "And how shall we defeat them?"

Leviathan nodded in acknowledgement. He turned to the orcs. "Tell us of your leader."

The smallest orc, the one who'd carried Sera, spoke for the group of captives. It was the most warped of them, with the face of an elderly human and the body of a hunchback. "My name is Janaway," the orc began, "and I have spent my adult life serving the Lumis cult and its founder, a man named Arthur Dennison."

"Dad!" Drew cried.

Janaway favored him with a nod. "Your father said you would be coming. We did not expect backup." He glanced at Leviathan and Sera in turn. "Though I daresay they will be welcome additions to the movement."

"Where is he?" Drew demanded. "Can you take me to him?"

"Such is our intent," Janaway responded, "but first I must ask that your companion remove and destroy her goggles."

#

Three hours later they stood before a stark black castle surrounded by an even blacker bog. The orcs had led the party deeper into the slough, away from the city and Camelot, taking pathways Drew could neither anticipate nor intuit. At times they'd seem to be backtracking only to emerge in terrain they'd clearly not traversed before. If he'd been online it would've taken half a moment's focus to set a breadcrumb path for their return. Under the circumstances Drew abandoned the line of thought easily enough. There would be no going back. He was on the way to see his father. He would finally get his answers.

The castle's drawbridge unwound with a massive chorus of creaking and moaning, as if it hadn't been opened in untold ages. It hit the ground with a muddy squelch.

"Home sweet home," Janaway quipped, stepping onto the bridge's massive beams.

"I want my sword back," Sera muttered as they traversed the drawbridge. The accent, along with her weapons and armor, had disappeared when she'd removed her goggles. Leviathan and Drew held the swords given by his rescuers and the orcs had retrieved their own, but Sera was for the nonce entirely weaponless.

"I don't think we're in danger," Drew said softly.

"It's not about that."

The inside of the castle was no different from its exterior: entirely black and lacking in ornamentation of any sort. Their footfalls did not echo but were rather absorbed by the darkness, swallowed into silence like an astronomical singularity. Algae torches illumed the hallways at intervals. Janaway led the procession up an interminable winding staircase.

They emerged at last in a belfry, the pinnacle of the black castle's lone observation tower. But where one might expect a church bell to hang there was instead a giant LED bulb attached to a revolving table. Curved metal sheeting surrounded it on three sides. It neither shone nor moved.

Morning light entered the belfry from the easternmost window. Set before it was a reclining chair facing the dawn. As Drew and his companions flowed into the little room the chair swiveled toward them. A wizened man with a dark complexion and curly black hair sat on it. He leaned forward and slowly pushed himself to his feet. "Greetings, noble questers. I have waited a long time for this moment."

"Dad!" Drew cried, pushing through the crowd.

The old man pressed his lips together and grimaced at the boy standing before him. "Andrew Arthur Dennison. I am sorry to have caused you such pain, son. I do not ask for your forgiveness, but merely a chance to explain."

#

CHAPTER 6

ARTHUR'S TALE

"You have been lied to," Arthur Dennison began, "from the very first moment of your lives."

The party of questers and orcs sat on the floor of the belfry. Arthur had retaken his seat on the recliner, Drew at his feet with an uncertain look on his face. A strange thing had happened as dawn grew into morning and the day's light returned: the orcs' twisted appendages and contorted features had settled into a less fantastical appearance. These were people after all, just far older and in worse health than anybody Drew had ever met.

"The system that was designed to save the world has imperiled its very existence," Arthur declared boldly, "this is the last stand of the human race."

"Amen," murmured the Loomies, who'd obviously heard the sermon before.

"When I was a kid the founders were still alive," Arthur continued. "The internet was young and malleable and not so complex that it couldn't be understood by the team of specialists who'd written its code in the first place. Our daily experience was getting constantly updated as the system's neural feedback learned more about humans' unique needs and desires.

"Eventually the time came when its processors outpaced theirs and the founders could no longer explain why it reached the conclusions it did. But they were all in accord about one thing, and that was that those conclusions *worked*.

"As the founders aged they delegated more and more responsibility to the algorithms. By the time the last member of the programming group lay on her deathbed they were responsible for 99.9% of the important decisions guiding human society. But even as my grandmother — for that's who the last member was — faded from this world, her thoughts were on that final tenth of a percent.

"As things stood nobody was in charge of this infinitesimal slice of destiny. It represented randomness, chance, the innate perversity of inanimate objects and the inherent complexity of the universe. But to my dying grandma it represented hope. It was a lever.

"She'd taught me to code when I was young. Perhaps she'd known it would come to this all along. In any case she spent her final breath relaying to me a password that would open a backdoor into the internet's neural network. That's how I've been able to keep us safe all these years. It's how I watched over you and your mother, Drew, and how my fellows were able to capture the mighty warrior princess beside you.

"I don't think my grandmother had an actual plan. She just foresaw the need to keep a human in the loop, even if it meant introducing the element of chaos into an otherwise orderly situation.

"At first I treated the backdoor like a game, a joke of sorts: I couldn't believe my dead grandmother had meant it to be used for anything important. Why would she? Like I said, the algorithms worked. Life was good. I was young and more focused on personal goals than abstract concepts like truth and reality.

"Her password did give me certain advantages, however. I could see out of other people's goggles. I could hear what they heard. I avoided more than one embarrassing encounter by scouting my peers in this way before engaging with them. And this was how I first learned of the danger the internet presented to our continued existence.

"There was this girl I had a thing for, her name was Vinge. This was before I met your mother, Andrew. I'll admit that I would play tourist in her goggles more often than might be considered prudent, had anyone discovered my vicarious activities. Anyway, one day Vinge wasn't in class so I switched over to her perspective. She was walking down a narrow alleyway. She stopped at a door and knocked. It opened and she stepped inside.

"What happened next confused me. She appeared to be covering her face with her hands. Then the background shifted abruptly. When she removed her hands I was hit with a moment of vertigo, for I was now looking directly at Vinge – but not the Vinge I knew so well. The picturesque girl with kinky hair and smooth brown skin that had just begun to develop curves was replaced with a gangly, awkward teen. That was when I finally understood. She had taken off her goggles.

"A man joined Vinge. He removed his goggles as well, and in an instant went from a glowering image of machismo to a portly gentleman with a sad smile and a receding hairline. They seemed to know each other, for they exchanged a moment of small talk. Then the man said something that has stuck with me to this day. He said, 'How is Simulumis treating you?'

"Vinge responded, 'Well you know. It's teetering.'

"'But holding.'

"'For the moment.'

"'Do you really think they'll ruin it?'

"'They always do.'

"'Then why don't we cut them off and be done with it?'

"'Soon enough, I suppose. It's just a shame. It feels so real. Who's to say they don't have human souls?'

"'Who's to say we do?'

"'Touché.'

"They sat together in companionable silence for maybe a minute. Then the man heaved a sigh and retrieved his goggles. He held them in one hand as he spoke. 'So long as they're looking inward they won't look out.'

"'That's the plan then. Monitor, assess, report back?'

"'For the time being,' the man laughed. 'That's a joke. You know, the proper time being the thing we're monitoring for.'

"'Jokes are supposed to be funny.'

"'Hey!'"

#

"Hold on a moment," Leviathan said, to Drew's relief. He'd been doing his best to follow the story, but his father was making a lot of assumptions about their understanding of matters that were frankly beyond him. Leviathan continued: "Are you saying the internet spawned independent artificial intelligences, or are Vinge and the man agents of the system itself?"

"And what's this about the proper time and cutting us off?" Sera added. "It was really unclear."

Arthur Dennison frowned at his audience. "You youngsters with your interruptions! When I was a child we knew how to listen to a story from start to finish. But nowadays everything has to be *interactive*." He nearly spat the word. "I've a mind to gag the lot of you."

"Artie!" One of the Loomies scolded. "Just tell the story."

Drew's father grimaced sheepishly.

#

"Where was I? Oh yes, Vinge's conversation. After that I watched her constantly. I didn't understand what it meant any more than you do in this moment, but I knew it was important. Sooner or later it would happen again. I'd just keep gathering information and eventually build it into a comprehensible model.

"What happened instead was that Vinge disappeared. I don't mean she went off the radar, or whatever the saying is. I mean that one day while I was watching her she took off her goggles and never put them back on.

"I waited in anticipation for school the next day. I arrived to the chat room early and took a seat behind her usual spot. The other desks filled but she never came. I didn't absorb anything from the lesson that day, just sat there and stared at the empty seat in front of me. And that night I resolved to find answers.

"I knew where she lived, more or less, from my observations. Once the sun set I excused myself with a feigned headache and crawled out my bedroom window. It was a short walk through the neighborhood. When I reached her street I kept to the edge of the sidewalk, away from the lights. I'd rendered myself into an elf for the mission: if anyone caught me I could claim I was on a quest or something equally trite.

"There weren't any lights on in her house. From the safety of the shadows I called up the commands that let me into my grandmother's secret backdoor. I pinged Vinge. Her goggles were still lying on the bedroom floor; from within their perspective I could just make out the street I was standing on through the window.

"I used my backdoor to ascertain that the house was empty. Then I strode confidently up the steps and went inside. Nobody used locks anymore. What I was doing was so far beyond the pale I could hardly believe it myself. But there I was, standing in the living room of my teenage crush, who didn't appear to be from the same plane of reality as myself. Not that anything in the house spoke of exotic origins. I wandered from room to room fitfully, examining photos and searching for clues in the family's personal touches. I watched myself pick up Vinge's goggles and carry them around. Nothing gave me any clue as to where she had gone.

"Finally, lacking any other productive ideas, I resolved to try on her goggles. Maybe the clue I was looking for could only be seen if I was wearing them. It was a slim chance, but I was out of options. I was grasping. So I closed my eyes and took off my goggles and set hers in their place.

"When I opened my eyes again nothing had changed. It was such a disappointment that I threw my own goggles to the floor in frustration. Something tinkled like broken glass. I swore, rapidly losing my cool, and fetched them up again. The nosepiece had separated from the lenses.

"And if that wasn't enough, Vinge's goggles were beginning to give me a headache; she must've suffered from astigmatism or something like it. I closed my eyes again and took them off. I considered trying to wedge my broken goggles in place for the walk home. Maybe it was my flaring temper, I don't know. I could've used either pair to dial emergency. Someone would've come with a new set of goggles. But instead I set both pairs down and willfully opened my eyes.

"Vinge's bedroom was empty. I mean completely empty. There wasn't so much as a bed frame on the floor. The walls were ancient lath and plaster with several peeling layers of paint in evidence. The rest of the house was the same – it did not appear anyone had lived in it for years. Vinge's entire existence was an illusion. The only evidence I had were the ill-fitting goggles. I retrieved them from her room and went outside.

"That was the first time in my life that I saw the world as it really was. Not a vibrant playground at all, not the cradle of a great civilization, no: we were living in filth and squalor. Our planet had been exploited and abandoned. And in that moment I understood.

"Simulumis isn't the virtual reality world we escape to with our goggles and the internet. It's the real world, our world, this one we're living in right now! Don't you get it? Vinge and her partner aren't artificial intelligences. *They're* the real people. They made *us*!"

CHAPTER 7

THEORY

That night, after a meager supper, Drew and his companions were led to guest quarters and left to their devices. A hearty fire burnt in a fireplace. Three pallets of straw had been set out for them. Otherwise the room was as barren as the rest of the castle.

"Is what he said even possible?" Sera asked at last, breaking the silence. "Are we literally bits and bytes in someone else's simulation?"

"The part I don't get is why," said Drew. "Why would they build it if they knew we would self-destruct?"

Leviathan cleared his throat. "The simulation theory," he recited from memory, "was first popularized by a gentleman named Nick Bostrom in 2003. He laid the groundwork for a thought experiment that goes like this – but remember, you have to think of it from his perspective. Pre-GI.

"By examining the rate of increase in processing capacity over the history of the existence of computers one can draw an exponential curve, which extrapolates to a future in which eventually humans would have virtually infinite processing power at their fingertips. In such a situation would it not stand to reason that these 'post-humans' would be interested in building an ancestry simulation to learn more about their origin?

"Based on these assumptions, Bostrom offered up a trilemma: three statements of which he claimed at least one must be true. First: no civilization ever attains post-human status. Second: no post-human civilization ever displays interest in running such a simulation. Third: all of existence is simulated except for the prime reality, and it's mathematically unlikely that ours is it."

They watched the flames dance about as they absorbed Leviathan's words.

"Vinge is from the future," Sera mused. "Or we're in her past. It's confusing."

"Maybe," said Leviathan. "Or maybe the theory is an over-simplification."

"All models are," Drew murmured, remembering Roberts' words.

"That's right," said Leviathan, rewarding Drew with a deferential nod. "The important thing is to select the right variables. Now, Bostrom just goes ahead and chooses ancestry simulations and I've always had a problem with that. The founders were as close to post-human as humanity ever got, but did they run ancestry simulations? No. They were forward thinkers. They had to be, because they were already aware of the mistakes their ancestors had made. They were trying not to make any more."

"Ooh!" Sera cried. "Future simulations!"

"It would explain what Vinge and company meant by 'they always ruin it,'" Drew put in.

"And once we've gone too far they cut us off."

"That's why my dad wants to shut off the internet!" Drew cried. "He knows our simulation is failing."

"The part I don't get," Leviathan said, "is why it hasn't happened yet. Wasn't that decades ago?"

"Maybe time runs differently in the real world," Sera said. "I mean the real real world. That is a weird thing to say."

"He said 'for the time being,'" Leviathan reminded her, "the proper time."

Drew yawned. "You guys can discuss it all night if you want. This is the proper time for me to get some sleep."

The last thing he heard before he zonked out was Sera saying, "if the only way to save this reality is by shutting down the internet, we are well and truly fucked."

#

"Wake up." Someone was shaking him.

Drew groaned, only to have fingers land lightly on his lips. "Don't wake the others!"

He opened his eyes. Janaway knelt over him, a veiled lantern hanging from one arm. "What gives?"

"I'm sorry to wake you," Janaway said, groveling as much as an orc could, "but there's something you need to see. Only you."

Something in the elderly guard's voice touched Drew. He sat up quietly and followed the stooped figure out of the room.

"I knew this was a cult when I joined," Janaway whispered as he led Drew through the castle. "I signed on for the benefits package, but I understood the job. We're orcs. We eat little girls and bash people's heads in. And that was fine as long as we stayed in our lane. Every once in a while some wannabe big-shot would come along and then we'd have a grand old time of leading him on before we killed him. But it wasn't like I was evil, you know? I was just playing my role.

"And then something changed. I remember exactly when it happened. Your father had just been returned to us from his eight year stay in prison. It was a time of joy and celebration. Our mission was trending, Lumis stock was up, recruiting had reached an all time high. There was talk of a grand gesture.

"That night we caroused beyond the limits of the dining hall's store of spirited beverages, and I was the unfortunate soul drafted with the task of fetching more from the cellar. I do not understand why the heaviest burdens fall on the weakest members of a group, but it is a pattern I have observed. In any case, as I was descending the spiral staircase into the underground portion of the castle – just ahead of where we're walking now – I chanced to hear the voice of your father murmuring in low tones. To this day I know not why I hid myself instead of calling out in companionable greeting, but that is what I did.

"Soon Sir Dennison emerged from the cellar into the moonlight cast by the sky windows of the spiral staircase. He was holding something, and though I was not able to make it out in detail I later determined it to be a scroll of sorts. It is hidden in the room yonder, and it is what I wish to show you."

Their ambulation had delivered them to a room of wine casks and machinery. It smelt of oak and lubricant. Janaway counted casks until he reached a particular one. He gestured for Drew's help, and the two pried its lid off together.

The inside was dry. At first it appeared empty, but at Janaway's insistence Drew reached an arm in and pulled out a scroll of sorts. It was hard to tell what kind in the dim light. They retreated to the staircase like his father must've, but the moon had either not risen or was currently out of phase.

Janaway unveiled his lantern. Drew held the scroll before it. A picture emerged in the flitting light: Drew as a baby boy, with his parents in the background, smiling. Drew flipped the scroll's page. Another picture, this one of just Drew and his mother. On the next page, another. Then another, and another. The entire scroll was a visual history of Drew's childhood.

"Sir Dennison gasped. 'How did they find me?' After that," Janaway finished in a hushed whisper, "Sir Dennison made no attempt toward a grand gesture. His efforts were pathetic at best, and though it was obvious to us all nobody dared bring it up to his face. Morale plummeted. We began losing members. Those of us you've met today are all that's left of what was once a grand movement. But that's not all."

Janaway led Drew back into the wine cellar and set his lantern on a cask near the one they'd opened. Its light shone inside. Drew leaned over and examined the depths. There was something else in it.

A pair of goggles.

#

Drew was returning to the guest quarters when he heard his friends voices.

"Forget it," Leviathan was saying through a yawn. "The quest can wait until after breakfast."

"I'm with you, grumpy," Sera said. "Something smells amazing."

"I get it. You called me a dwarf, and it's funny because I'm really big."

"No, I called you grumpy because you're grumpy!"

"Wake up!" Drew called out, and then, because he was feeling a little grumpy himself, added, "it's a beautiful morning."

Leviathan roared in dismay.

"You're asking for a smack to the head," Sera warned.

Drew sobered as he remembered the last time he'd earned one. Fate had not allowed him to collect that debt. "I have something to tell you." He laid out the night's conversation with Janaway, ending with the discovery of the scroll and the goggles.

"So where is the little sneak?" Sera asked when he'd finished talking. "Probably listening to us right now!"

"I don't think Janaway is the problem," Drew said.

Leviathan was nodding in concern.

"What?" Sera said, her head flitting between them wildly. "What don't I understand?"

Leviathan took pity on her. "We think Arthur Dennison stopped trying to bring down the internet after Vinge emotionally blackmailed him with the pictures, reminding him of the consequences to his family if he did."

"Like they'd hurt Drew or something?"

"Like they'd shut off Simulumis and erase him from existence!"

"Oh. Well fuck."

"Yeah."

They sunk into a gloomy silence. Eventually the smell of breakfast overrode their existential dilemma and they tromped out to the dining hall. Janaway was just finishing his. One of the other orcs served them and they retired to a table in the corner.

They'd nearly polished off the food on their plates when Sera snapped her fingers. "I know why it didn't make sense," she said, "there was a piece missing. I mean – with all due respect – Arthur is a fanatic; he must've known that shutting down the internet would cause untold suffering in the short run. I couldn't understand why the pictures of Drew would've changed his mind. And I don't think they did."

"Now I'm not following you," Leviathan said, and Drew nodded in agreement.

"It wasn't the pictures," Sera explained patiently. "It was the fact that he received them at all. He said, *how did they find me?* Vinge's people made contact with him!"

Leviathan dropped his hands onto the table with a thud. "Who's the smart one now? Sera, that's brilliant! That means they've been tracking him. He knows he's being watched."

"Not only that," Sera added, "he knows that shutting the internet off is a dead end. For both worlds."

"So what *is* he trying to do?"

"I think I can answer that," Drew said. He glanced about furtively, but the dining hall had emptied. He reached into a pocket and withdrew Vinge's goggles and set them on the table. "He's trying to talk to God."

#

They retreated to their quarters to discuss next steps. Leviathan wanted to confer with Arthur, but Sera thought he might grow volatile when he learned they'd pilfered Vinge's goggles. Drew didn't know what to think. So much had happened in such a short time. So many theories had blown though his mind, and yet it seemed like the most fantastical of them all was turning out to be the true one. Multiple levels of simulations. Future casting. Shadowy agents fine tuning reality. It was hardly a wonder his father wanted to communicate with them.

"I think we should put them on," he said abruptly. "The goggles, I mean."

Sera and Leviathan stared at him in surprise.

"At one point it was useful," he reminded them. "You can see things that aren't there. Which is, in a way, exactly what we need right now. To find a solution we can't see."

It took a while to convince them. Drew was the first to admit it wasn't a plan so much as a roll of the dice; but nobody else seemed to have a better idea, and when he pointed out that this might be their only chance to try it – if they brought Arthur into the fold he may very well take the goggles from them – they relented at last, first Sera and finally Leviathan, though the reluctant giant made them promise they would divulge everything to Arthur once this 'wildly irresponsible experiment' was concluded.

Then came the problem of who should wear them. Leviathan wanted no part in it. Drew was game, but Sera argued that her astigmatism made her a better fit. Neither boy wanted to put her at risk. Sera laughed in their faces.

"I've killed two hundred bosses," she reminded them, "without magic."

That settled it. Drew handed the goggles over.

As she was preparing to insert them into her eye sockets Leviathan said, "Remember, we won't be able to see or hear what you're seeing and hearing. You'll have to describe it for us."

"Roger," Sera muttered. "Play by play commentary coming up." She wiggled the goggles into place and her posture immediately straightened. "Milord," she gasped, and curtsied at nobody in particular.

Drew and Leviathan exchanged a glance. Without speaking they shifted positions to flank Sera on both sides, the typical placement for bodyguards or servants or whatever role required of them by the fantasy she was experiencing.

"Oh, them?" Sera said, as if on cue. She began prancing out of the room. "Merely my entourage. They are tragically mute. Come on, boys, this train won't carry itself!"

Drew and Leviathan followed behind her, seething.

Sera's invisible guide led them through the nearly abandoned castle. Once Drew heard the low murmurs of orcs but nobody challenged them, not even when they opened a side door off the royal kitchen and departed the safety of the castle walls. Outside was just as they'd left it: boggy and gross. But Sera led them unwaveringly through the muck until they arrived at a spot that looked exactly like every other spot.

"Here lies a glowing portal!" Sera announced. "Inside it does exist a pocket universe, in which the rules and rhythms of this land hold no sway."

"Let's do this," Drew said. Leviathan nodded grimly.

On the count of three, the party leapt into the mud.

#

"We have emerged on the outskirts of a marketplace," Sera narrated. "Rows of tents line a street which may have once been paved but is now buried beneath layers of grass and sediment and river rock. Beyond that weeds have grown ten feet tall and stretch to the edges of a great canyon."

Leviathan shook his head. "You know what I don't get? In the old classics, when the heroes went to a magic fairy tale land, the world was awesome! You know what I'm saying? Oz and Narnia, the Land, Fillory, T'Rain, SAO and the Oasis... even Hogwarts was cool in its own way. But what do we get? Endless forests and an overgrown garden." He sighed. "Oh well. At least it's not derivative."

"Mind yourselves!" Sera cried.

The boys looked about reflexively, but nothing appeared imminently dangerous.

"You're blocking the path!" she said, gesturing to the side. "Noble sir, I beg leave for my servants. Yes, they have clouds in their brains. Yes, I will tell them myself."

Drew and Leviathan followed Sera's gesturing arms reluctantly.

"That's better," she said. "Now we can watch the parade. Will you look at them? Elves of all sorts, and dwarves, and warriors and princesses, wizards and merchants and giants and trolls. There's even a centaur! And Halflings and hobgoblins and hobbits, naiads and dryads and satyrs and fauns, munchkins and monkeys and brownies and fairies and imps!"

Drew directed a look at Leviathan. "You happy now?"

"Oh, did I do that?"

"Hush!" Sera called. "Listen to the barker! Can you hear him? He's welcoming us to the marketplace of Balal, where we can find everything our hearts desire. The richest of desserts? Easy! The finest of cheeses? Done! The most beautiful men and women and non-binary people to grace the face of the earth are right here, but we will have to woo them with our charm as well as our purses, for nobody's body should be bought or sold against their will! Don't be shy, the barker says, tell him your pleasure and he'll point you to it. The best ales in the land? Look no further, my fine gent! Are you seeking your long lost cousin on your mother's side? Our fortune tellers know where to find them! Spells, weapons, armor? Check check check! You've come to the right place, the only place, step this way and spend your money... just don't forget to go home!"

"Don't tip the barker," Drew whispered to Sera. "The merchant rhythms will tag you as a newbie and all the prices go up by ten percent."

"How do you know?" Leviathan wondered.

Drew made a face.

"Prices are of no concern to me," Sera boasted. "I'm rich. I've killed–"

"Two hundred bosses!" Drew and Leviathan finished her sentence simultaneously. "We know!"

Now Sera made a face. "Come on. Let's go find a backdoor."

They followed her up and down the slough, listening to her descriptions. At first it was exciting to hear her describe the exotic faces and foods and smells and noises, the foreign dishes that were proffered for her to sample. She described a bunraku play featuring dueling puppeteers; a slam poet eviscerating Shakespeare in iambic pentameter; a faun wedding in which they cheered for the newlywed goat couple. But Drew tired of the narration quicker than he would've thought possible. His legs grew heavy and his back sore and he began lagging behind.

After a minute Leviathan noticed and slowed his pace to join his friend. "Man," he said, "your girlfriend's a real hard-ass."

"Not my girlfriend," Drew said shortly. "I doubt she'll ever be."

"You could try talking to her."

"Yeah."

"Uh, does *yeah* mean that's a good idea, or *yeah* that obviously a good idea and you've already tried it?"

"Sorry. The first one. It's just hard, you know. I have these memories I want to share with her but that's going to remind her she doesn't have them."

"Maybe," said Leviathan. "Or maybe it will help. She seems very set on determining whose reality we're in."

"When did you become Doctor Love?" Drew scowled. He picked up his pace, leaving Leviathan behind.

#

The primary reason for pocket quests was to give struggling players a place to play games of chance and win coin, and to then spend that coin on items that would help them reach their goal. Balal was probably connected to a thousand places on the internet. Drew had known not to talk to the barker because he'd been to similar markets; Leviathan could joke all he wanted, but Drew was sure his friend had visited them too. It was all a part of leveling up.

He didn't much care about leveling up anymore. He just wanted to finish the task at hand so they could move on to the next task, which hopefully would make a lot more sense than what they were doing now. It was strange to think how most of his life had consisted of this exact sort of thing. Shadow play. It sure seemed silly from the outside.

Sera had stopped walking while he woolgathered. "We're being followed," she said.

Drew resisted the urge to look behind them. "By whom?"

But instead of addressing him Sera made eye contact with a stump. "Hail, fair imp, but do not come any closer. My entourage has not bathed in a fortnight."

"Hey!" protested Drew.

"It's no lie," admitted Leviathan. "But hush up. Something's at play."

"No thank you," Sera was saying, "I don't want to buy any free advice. How does that even work? Pay you and find out? Ha! I can spot a devil's bargain when I hear one!" She cocked her head and listened. "We need to watch out for a bully? Fine. How much for your sage advice? What are you talking about, you don't have anything for sale! Hey, where are you going?" She shook her head. "Imps."

Drew rubbed his head. Nothing made sense. It felt like the internet had started to take things literally, like it was learning human language for the first time and had built a card house of impossibilities on grammatical paradoxes that could never coexist in a sound and functioning universe. They might as well take everything literally from this point on as well.

Wait a moment. That was it! Before they'd entered into Sera's magic portal she'd said the rules and rhythms of the real world – or Simulumis, anyway – didn't hold sway here. He took a deep breath.

"Uh, guys," he said, "I think I was wrong. We do have to tip the barker."

#

"Welcome to the Marketplace of Balal! Here you can find everything your heart desires. The richest of desserts? Easy! The finest of cheeses? Done! The most beautiful men and-"

"Just give him the money," Drew interrupted. "This is taking all day."

Sera shot him a look but opened an invisible purse and flipped something into the air.

"The barker has caught my coin. He's wearing a pinstripe suit over his emaciated husk. His breath reeks of onions and death. In one hand he holds a loudspeaker and the other, a cigar. He's telling me to lay down my weapons and take up the art of nursing. Now I'm telling him to insert his microphone so far up his rectum that it meets his cigar. I do believe I've made an enemy."

"Fight!" Drew cried maniacally.

"Cancel that, he's back to barking. This NPC has a limited rhythm."

"Well, that was a bust." Leviathan kicked at the mud fitfully.

They loped away from the market's entrance, not that Drew could tell the difference. They'd been traversing the same stretch of bog for hours. He was weary and disheartened.

His insight about taking things literally hadn't panned out. But what else could the imp have meant? Pay and find out. Okay. Sera had paid the barker. What were his exact words? He'd told Sera to lay down her weapons and take up the art of nursing.

"Hey Sera. Have you seen anything like a medical tent?"

#

Sera stood before the med tent door, Drew and Leviathan slightly behind her. She drew her sword and lodged it in the muck, its handle swaying slowly from side to side.

"Be careful what you say," Drew whispered. "No metaphors until we're out of here."

They stepped across the threshold.

"'Tis bigger than I thought possible," Sera said. "But where's the doctor? There's not even a shaman or a faith healer. And just the one bed. With a troll in it."

They crowded around Sera, somehow claustrophobic even though the tent was invisible to them. "What's wrong with it?" Leviathan asked.

Sera shook her head. "Despite the barker's urging, I am not a nurse. But anyone can see this troll is suffering from a wart outbreak. They have not been tended in some time. He is drooling as well, it appears his bedpan needs to be changed, and his legs seem atrophied. That would explain the wheelchair."

Drew and Leviathan exchanged a significant look. The giant whispered, "sounds like our old nemesis is about to bite the- is about to die," he amended.

"Then he can fain give us his blessing!" cried Sera.

"I get it," Drew groaned. "We have to *look out for* a bully. As in help him."

"I'll search the stores," Sera said. She began rummaging about in the mud, saying things contentedly like *IV bags* and *sterile supplies* and other useful items one might expect to find in an emergency medical tent in a fairy tale marketplace in a pocket universe.

One determined hour later, she stood back to describe her work. She'd swapped the goblin's IV bag for a fresh one. She'd misted his warty body with soothing essential oils. She'd even, eyes averted at all costs, replaced his gown with a fresh one — actually two, cleverly repurposed into a single piece that covered both his sides and tucked under the gurney's edges.

None of it seemed to have made any difference.

"I can't stand waiting any longer," Leviathan grumbled. "I'm taking a nap. Wake me if he wakes up."

Sera didn't answer. She'd seated herself on the ground and was scanning her inventory.

Drew sat down as well. The day had grown hotter and hotter. His face was pouring with sweat, his body shaking. He closed his eyes and ran through everything that had happened in the pocket universe, desperate for any clue that would tell them how to proceed.

"Sera," he said at last, "what was in the IV?"

After a moment she replied. "A beta blocker. Is that good? I told you I'm not a nurse!"

"No, it's fine," Drew said hurriedly. "You did the right thing. I'm just wondering... Levi," he said, using his friend's real name deliberately, "what was it your dad took for his heart condition? Wasn't it a beta blocker?"

The slumbering giant nodded. "High blood pressure. It calmed him down."

Sera was already fiddling with the IV bag. "This guy's a little too calm." She squeezed the drip valve shut. Then, taking care not to touch the troll's warts, she pulled the needle from his arm and set it aside.

"And now, for the second time in as many hours," she said, "we wait."

Drew groaned and lay back on the ground.

#

In his delirium or in his dreams, Drew watched Flabs wake from his stupor. Sera cranked up his bed so the goblin could sit. He surveyed his small audience with a look of consternation. "What the hell are you three doing?"

"Saving your sorry ass," Sera retorted. She wiped the drool from his face.

"This isn't a joke. You guys could get hurt, and who would help you then? Me?" He laughed bitterly. "I can't even help myself."

"We don't need your help," said Drew. "We need your blessing."

Flabs laughed again. It devolved into an ugly cough. "My blessing," he said once he was able to speak freely, "is worth less than the air in my windpipes. Don't you understand? I'm a hypocrite!

"I can't stop thinking about the things I've done," Flabs continued, his eyes held fast on Drew, "the ways I hurt you. The time I wasted. When we could've been friends! Instead I let you fend for yourself in a hostile world. Worse, I was part of that hostility. And look where it's gotten me."

"Hey, whoa, it feels like we're getting personal here," Sera said. "We were never gonna be friends."

"I get it," said Flabs, though his demeanor sagged at her statement. "I have a lot to make up for. Don't worry about it. I've found a niche here. It's nothing glamorous, and that's exactly what I need right now."

Drew tucked his hands in his pockets. "Maybe I'll see you back in town someday."

"About that," said Flabs, "if by some chance you make it back and I don't, will you tell everyone what happened? Will you tell them I changed?"

Drew promised to honor his request. They shook hands somberly.

"Well then," said Flabs, "I guess there's nothing more to do than send you off with my blessing."

"Finally!" crowed Leviathan, leaping to his feet. "Can we go now?"

CHAPTER 8

COUNCIL

The sun had angled below the forest's canopy by the time Drew awoke for real. Sera and Leviathan were sitting nearby, speaking in hushed whispers. Drew sat up and rubbed his eyes. "How'd it go?" he said, "did you win us a clue?"

Sera favored him with a sour look. "Not funny."

"What do you mean? We got Flabs' blessing!"

Leviathan scrutinized his groggy friend. "Arthur's blessing, you mean."

"Wait." Drew was growing more confused by the second. "What?"

Sera sighed. "While we were waiting for Flabs to wake your father interrupted us. Don't you remember? You talked to him!"

"My dream," said Drew, groaning. "I thought it was real!" He relayed the conversation he'd had with Flabs.

"That's pretty much how it went down," Leviathan said. "But it wasn't Flabs, it was your dad. And he took the goggles back."

Leviathan and Sera lapsed into silence.

Drew watched them for a long minute. Something turned over in his mind. "Why didn't he bring us back with him?" he asked. "Why did he show up and take the goggles, then leave us out here? After all the trouble it took to get us there in the first place."

"We stole the goggles," Leviathan repeated.

Sera shook her head. "Did you hear him? He was so full of remorse for leaving there's no way he'd abandon Drew again without a good reason."

"It wasn't safe," Drew translated, "he was still protecting me."

"Holy crap," said Leviathan, putting the pieces together.

"My dad knew he was compromised. He had to stay away from me and mom to keep us safe. But when he saw me take off my goggles he knew it was time to bring me into the loop, so he set the trap with Sera here as bait. Sorry about that."

She shrugged, half smirking. "Good to know they cheated. I'm not losing my edge."

"But when the first thing we did was nab the goggles and flee the castle, my dad must've known he had to get to us before Roberts."

"Who I think was Vinge's companion all along," Sera added.

#

Night fell upon the glum group of adventurers as they attempted to find their way out of the forest bog. They'd lapsed into silence after several attempted conversations had devolved into bickering. Drew's legs felt like deadweights. He was on the verge of calling a halt for the night when a flickering light appeared in the distance.

Leviathan hollered. Sera elbowed him in the ribs, cutting off his cry. "What gives?"

"Prudence suggests we determine the light's source before availing ourselves of it," she said, lapsing into internet talk. "It may well be foe or friend."

"Whatever," the giant grumbled. "Like we have a choice."

But he ceased arguing and stood silently with Sera and Drew, watching the flickering light wind its way through the murk and gloom. It wasn't heading directly at them but close enough. Soon they could hear footfalls and a mumbling grumble, though too faint to make out distinct words. Then the light coalesced into a lantern and the stooped form of Janaway could be seen holding it before himself as he picked his way through the bog.

"Not cool," the orc was mumbling to itself, "not cool at all. Skulking about the woods at night, sure, capturing maidens and errant questers, I can do that. But nobody said I would have to betray my own people! No thank you, mister whomever you are. I'll take my chances on my own."

"He's on our side," Drew whispered. Before his companions could respond he stood up and stepped into the light. "Hail, Janaway!"

The hunchbacked orc nearly dropped his lantern in surprise. "Master Drew!" he gasped. "And Masters Levi and Sera as well. You must flee from here. We've been invaded!"

#

Sunrise found the party marching in single file through the slough, Janaway in the lead. They'd cleared several miles in the night, the orc's lantern and guidance a boon to navigation. Not that any of the younger members of the party had a clue as to where they were headed. All they knew was what Janaway knew: two bumblebee drones had emerged from the sky to snatch Arthur and subdue his faithful. The orcs had been interrogated and propositioned: they would be set free if they promised to return to human society and spread harmful lies about the Lumis cult.

"A promise made under duress is non-binding," Janaway had assured them, "Not a one of us ever intended to backslide."

Shortly after the sun rose Janaway took their bearings and executed a sharp direction change. Now they were crossing the fingers of the slough instead of paralleling them. It was tough hiking, and more than once Drew nearly called for a rest. But none of his companions seemed winded so he held his peace and kept struggling forward. Then the trees thinned and the sky opened and they were abruptly back at the river.

Camelot was nowhere in view. Neither was Gabby's island of lost souls.

In mutual silent agreement the party made camp near the river bank, concealed enough by the forest that searching drones would not spot them. Drew and Leviathan collected firewood while Sera whittled a branch into a spear and squatted by the river's edge, searching for dinner. Janaway gathered a ball of duff and tinder and built a tipi out of the logs the boys had collected. Drew let him work the flint and steel. In a short moment they had a cheery blaze going. Sera returned with a single frog thrashing on her spear.

"Oho!" cried Leviathan. "I thought you were Maid Marian but you're Robin Hood!"

Sera dropped the struggling amphibian onto the ground. "Maybe I'm Robin Hood, but you're cleaning it."

#

After dinner they had a council of war.

"This is how I see it," Sera said, "tell me if I've missed anything. In the real world, one level up from here, it's still the Great Interruption. Vinge and Roberts *are* the founders, but they haven't rebuilt the internet at all. What they've done is run future simulations to find the best way forward for themselves. Only none of them are working. And so they've entered into their own simulations to tweak the parameters, guiding us toward a future in which we don't go extinct."

"Or searching for one," Drew put in. "They don't seem to have a better plan than we do."

Sera acknowledged his comment with a nod. "Roberts lied to motivate you to find your father. He said he'd put the entire resources of his consortium at the Lumis cult's disposal. But all he really cared about was closing Arthur's backdoor. He may have even let Arthur out of prison in order to lead him to it!"

"Why is that so important?" Leviathan mused.

Drew snapped his fingers. "'So long as they're looking inward they won't look out!'"

Sera understood. "They don't want us to know we're living in a simulation."

"Maybe they're afraid we'll get out."

"Maybe it's happened before and inevitably leads to failure."

"Maybe understanding the technology ruins the magic." This from Janaway, who'd been following the conversation with a look of bemusement on his face. "Seriously, kids.

Look around yourselves. The world is dying. Who but fringe outliers like ourselves would choose to spend their days here when the internet offers such comfort and security? How can anyone in their right mind claim this world – Simulumis – is a better option?"

"But if we abandon it for the internet," said Drew glumly, "it will fail. And they'll shut us down."

"But even if we found a way to turn off the internet the simulation would fail anyway, because nobody knows how to live offline anymore." Leviathan pointed out.

"So we can't shut it down and we can't use it," Sera summarized, "and the only way to secure our future is to find one for the real world. Is that accurate?"

Janaway uttered a dry chuckle. "You don't take half measures, you don't."

#

The fire had burned to embers when the waxing moon rose above the horizon, lighting the campsite by degrees. Leviathan lay spooned around half of the fire, snoring. Janaway had wrapped himself in his cloak. Sera and Drew sat beside each other, their shoulders almost touching.

"Tell me about the other me," Sera said.

Drew studied her profile like he might never have the chance again. "She was fearless," he said, "so much that it scared me. She never backed down from a challenge."

"How did she die?"

Drew scowled at the memory. "We were trying to cross the river." He shook his head ruefully. "Waking up alone was the worst feeling of my life. All the things I wanted to tell you. I'd never been so happy as the days we spent together. I could've stayed there forever with you. I should've said something and I didn't, and it's amazing and wonderful that you're here again but you don't remember and in a way it's worse because I have these memories and you don't." He took a breath, relieved that he'd finally expressed himself but terrified of what she might say next.

Sera took her time responding. "You lost her while trying to help her, even though it wasn't part of the quest you were on. Then you went back and rescued me from the orcs. Why?"

Drew wanted to say, isn't it obvious? I'm in love with you! But the words wouldn't leave his lips.

"Was she more real to you than I am?" Sera asked quietly.

"More real?" Drew blurted. "We've just discovered that we've been living in a virtual reality inside of a simulation, and you're worried about what I think is real? Girl, as far as I'm concerned you're the same person I've had a crush on since first grade. I'm just glad for a second chance to enjoy your company."

They lapsed into silence, their shoulders still not quite touching. Tomorrow was coming, and whether they were ready for it or not they would have to face its unique challenges and opportunities.

Drew was drifting off when Sera spoke again. "Did we kiss?"

"In my dreams," he murmured, "you're a great kisser. Not that I have anything to compare it to."

Sera giggled. "Is this how you imagined it would happen?"

Drew opened his eyes in surprise. She pressed her face into his.

Not many people get to fall in love with the same person twice. But that's what happened for Drew, and he was determined not to lose her again. He lay awake long after Sera succumbed to the wandering sandman's pixie dust, plotting the course of future events in his mind, searching for a thread that would bind the disparate realities of the simulation and the real world or whatever shape existence actually took on.

He was still searching when the light returned.

#

CHAPTER 9

MAROONED

"This is Camelot?" Leviathan shook his head in dismay.

They'd crossed the bridge and walked right through the great castle's gates without as much as a challenge from the guards, who were all occupied with pitchforks and wheelbarrows, scooping up the prodigious loads of camel poop that littered the ground. The royal beasts wore robes of glittering greens and purples, and one dignified dromedary in particular sported a golden halo atop its phlegmatic head. This noble ungulate sat atop a dais of hard crusted sand, its legs tucked under itself daintily as it snacked on grains and fresh grasses strewn before it.

Drew smirked. "I thought you liked literal interpretations."

"This is not that," the giant declared. "This is a bad pun. Camel Lot!" Leviathan shook his head.

"It doesn't matter," said Drew, surveying the scene, "there's enough people for this to work."

They pushed past the throne room, more of a zoo display than a functioning court, and entered the castle's public square. In the middle water poured from a marble camel's mouth into a staged oasis, where birds and calves splashed gleefully. People and older ungulates lounged together or separately. Small groups had formed around a juggler and a storyteller.

Drew guided them to an open area near the castle wall where the sun's rays shone the brightest. Leviathan got down on his hands and knees. Sera and Janaway helped Drew crawl onto his back and stand up. This caused a bit of a stir, so Drew began his speech forthwith.

"Good people of Camel-Lot!" he cried, his voice as firm as he could make it. "I am here to bestow a quest upon you, a mission that has the potential to affect the very fabric of the universe we live in!" As he spoke Sera and Janaway urged people closer with gentle gestures and welcoming smiles. "Do you feel lost?" Drew continued. "Are you stuck in a rut? Do you want to go home but *it's not there anymore*? Well, you're not alone! We're all locked out– or locked in, depending on your point of view – and the only thing we can do about it is come together! Who's with me?"

The small crowd that had gathered as Drew spoke watched silently. Nobody answered his question. A few murmured amongst themselves but most just stood there, waiting for him to say more.

"This isn't the real world," Drew said, grasping for the straw that would break the camel's back, "I'm calling you to join us today in removing your goggles and returning to reality! There we'll make the world so beautiful that even God will be jealous!"

He paused to catch his breath. The crowd had grown marginally bigger. One guy in the front row, a dullard with a pitchfork, scratched his head in concentration.

"You want us to logout?" he asked Drew.

"Yes!" Drew cried, "if enough people do it together then maybe we can begin to heal some of the harm our neglect has caused."

Another of the camel attendants, this one standing beside a barrow of manure, spoke up. "So what you're saying is, you want to gather people into an army... and not attack anyone?"

Drew nodded, though it wasn't how he would have put it.

"That don't sound healing," said the dullard, "it sounds like a waste of time!"

The crowd murmured in agreement and began firing off logistical questions. *How long would we logout for? Will meals be provided? Are camping spaces going to be reserved or is it a first come first serve type of situation? Should I bring sunscreen?*

Drew's spirits dropped. He wasn't reaching them at all. Nobody seemed to care about anything outside of their own little bubble. It was like the entire world had adapted to the simulation, like they *preferred* it, and who were these Loomies to come and say things should go back to the way they were before? How could the past be better than the present, or more important than the future? And anyway, wouldn't logging out cause just as many problems as it would solve?

The pulpit was for preaching, not debating philosophy. But Drew didn't have the rhetoric to say the words that would turn a mob into a cudgel, a massively multiplayer pawn to wield for his own purposes. Which wasn't the point anyway. He wanted the people to want what he wanted.

"It's not a party," he snapped. "This is serious business! Don't you want a future?"

The murmur subsided at his outburst. Everyone was staring at him. Drew groped for words to fill the void. "We need to work together," he said. "That's the only way we'll ever get this done. Now come on, put down your pitchforks and your goggles! We have a job to do!"

Their response was less than enthusiastic. Instead of rallying behind his words the people in the crowd murmured in confusion. Finally the dullard said what they were all thinking.

"Uh, what job would that be now then?"

#

Drew called for a strategic pause to the campaign. They retreated to a campsite out of nose range of the dung piles that littered the countryside around the castle.

"This isn't working," he said bluntly. "We're trying to hit a home run but we've never even swung a baseball bat. Hell, we don't even know which direction the pitch is coming from. We could be so far out in left field... I'm out of metaphors, guys. I think we need help."

Sera stared at him in mock concern. "Like, literally?"

"Are you asking if I'm literally out of metaphors or if I really think we need help with our campaign? Because the answer is yes."

She placed her hand on his. "I'm proud of you for admitting you need help. But, who is there to ask? In case you forgot the internet is unsafe."

Drew turned his hand over to grip Sera's. Then he shot a look at Leviathan. "There is one person we could ask."

#

They would return to Gabby's island and press the sybil for information. She must represent some sort of nexus point, or was herself a vessel capable of transmitting information between worlds. In any case she was their best chance to gain intelligence, now that they had a sense of the relevant questions to ask.

There was just one problem.

"I can't go with you," Janaway said, "I'm not to be trusted."

The group assured their orc companion they did trust him; he'd proved his mettle time and again. They were not concerned he would turn against them.

But Janaway shook his head sadly and explained. "I know your plan. They can force it from me. And if I learn what the sybil tells you they can take that from me as well."

"None of us are safe from such an ambuscade," Sera pointed out.

"Ay, but the three of you are young and strong. You can protect each other. I will fall behind, and if you try to save me we will all be caught."

"But if we leave you now that's gonna happen anyway," Leviathan protested.

Janaway nodded solemnly. He drew himself as erect as his hunchback would allow. "That is why you have to kill me."

At this the questers protested passionately, but Janaway held firm. "I will respawn like your fearless warrior princess," he said, "and I will not remember a thing. It is for the best."

Drew continued to object long after his companions went quiet. There must be alternatives if only they would put their heads together to find them, he insisted. But eventually he was the only one speaking, for Janaway had joined Sera and Leviathan in silence. Drew threw his arms into the air and stalked off. He wandered down to the river and began chucking stones into the water. The crazy hadn't stopped since that first moment when he'd taken off his goggles and been seen by Roberts. All he'd wanted to do was find his father, and now he was caught up in a plot that could result in his world blinking out of existence – and his wasn't even the real world anyway! It felt like he'd taken on the fight for all of humanity. But what was *he* fighting for?

At length Leviathan joined him. His friend had no problem waiting until he was ready to talk. They threw rocks and the occasional stick into the flowing current. There was a soothing rhythm to it. Heave, arc, plop. Heave, arc, plop. Watch the concentric circles fight the current. Sometimes their waves combined with a pleasing pattern of interference. This made Drew think of all the simulations the founders must be running simultaneously, veritable living universes created not by some omniscient being but by a desperate group of humans seeking a path through the chaos, a future in which their mistakes would not result in the death of every living person on the planet.

In light of those stakes, one man's memories of the past few days seemed a small sacrifice to make.

Leviathan lifted a rock the size of his head. He hefted it into the shallows, causing water to splash across the bank. The rock split in two as it hit the bottom, a piercing crack emanating from the river.

"That's what happens if we fail," Drew said grimly.

#

They shook Janaway's hand in turn, first Drew and then Leviathan and at last Sera, who abandoned the ancient ritual for a wholehearted hug. The elderly orc patted her back awkwardly.

"Don't you worry about me one bit," he assured them. "Just focus on your quest."

He'd requested to die as painlessly as possible, and to that end they'd searched until Sera identified a stand of hemlock among the Queen Anne's lace and foxglove and mullein that battled for light in the interstitial zone between the river and the forest.

Janaway had made tea and drunk it some time ago. Now the kids sat with him and waited for the poisonous herb to do its work. His breathing had grown ragged and his hands had begun to shake.

"I don't regret anything," he whispered. "I'd do it all the same if I had to do it again."

"Word to that," said Leviathan.

"I helped, didn't I? I made things better?"

They assured him that he had.

A tear slipped out of Drew's eye. "One for all, and all for one," he misquoted. "I don't know about you guys, but I don't want anything to do with a reality you're not a part of. And that goes for everyone else, even the Flabs and the Crabs; all the players and the NPCs living a life in their own right. They deserve existence too."

Sera made a fist. "United we stand!"

Leviathan rolled his eyes. "Divided we fall. This is so cheesy."

"Am I the fourth musketeer then?" Janaway whispered. "Groovy!"

Then he died.

#

The best way to get back to Gabby's island, it turned out, was to head further upriver to the town of Salmon Hill, so named for a fishlike ridge of land the river wound through on its way to the ocean, and charter a ferry. The port lay at the tail end of the narrows, a muddy affair with rough-hewn log pillars tentatively keeping the pier above water.

Sera negotiated with a gregarious ferry captain, who was more than delighted to provide them with portage to the island of lost souls, just so long as they agreed that neither she nor her crew would be expected to set foot on land.

"It's an otherworldly place," the outspoken captain explained as the ferry pushed away from shore. She chewed a foul smelling root that hung from her mouth for the duration of their time onboard. "All sorts wash up there, human flotsam from strange dimensions. Some of them are even *dead*."

Drew and Leviathan exchanged a look.

"This one time, instead of coming to us, some enterprising fools tried to build a raft to cross the river on their own. It didn't hold together, of course, and both of the passengers – young lovers as it were – plunged to their death. One of their bodies was found downriver wedged amongst tree roots. The other washed up on the island. Legend has it they're still haunting it today." The captain cackled. "But if that's where you want to go, suit yourselves!"

Drew was starting to feel nauseous. He couldn't talk. He gripped the ferry's safety rail until his knuckles turned white. Leviathan patted his back gently.

"What's with him?" the captain said, spitting a lump of root overboard. "Looks like he's seen a ghost."

"Don't listen to her," Leviathan said.

"Just... can you get her to stop talking?" Drew whispered.

Leviathan looked at Drew with forlorn, empathetic eyes.

Sera stepped to the rescue. As nonchalantly as the flu, she climbed up to the poop deck and seated herself directly in the captain's line of sight. "What's your name, captain?"

The grizzled woman rumbled with displeasure. "It's Burdock, and I'll thank you to stay off the poop."

"Cap'n Burdock, has anybody spoken to you about the cult of Lumis?"

#

Drew and Sera rowed the ferry's jolly boat to shore while Leviathan waded behind, making sure they stayed out of the currents that broke against the island's bow.

"Well, at least we have a way to reach the mainland if Burdock maroons us," Sera said under her breath.

"Fair trade if we never have to hear her again."

"I'm sure she'd say the same thing," Sera giggled. "Nobody likes an evangelist. Shit! I've become an evangelist."

"If there's a better way to do this, we're about to learn what it is," Drew assured her.

They grounded on the beach fronting the dunes that sheltered Gabby's lean to. The sun was shining and a light wind blew offshore. Drew pointed out landmarks as he ran up the sandy slope, urging his friends to hurry.

"That's what's left of my fire. Over this dune is where I woke up. Come on, she's probably there right now!"

They crested the dune and came to an abrupt halt, bumping into each other clumsily. There was no lee. There was no lean to. The forest extended to the edge of the sand, thick hickory and cypress and dogwoods crowding together above a tenuous floor of muck and mire that offered passage for no being, corporeal or otherwise.

Across the water, Cap'n Burdock cackled with glee.

#

They ate a picnic lunch of dried fish and crackers, then gathered driftwood until they had enough fuel to last the night. When it became obvious they weren't returning Burdock hoisted anchor and the ferry slowly tacked upstream.

None of them seemed to mind. They'd grown solemn as the evening progressed. By the time their fire was lit and they'd settled down to watch its dancing flames nobody had spoken for an hour. Drew and Sera sat apart by mutual understanding. Leviathan stayed awake longer than normal. They kept their backs to the river and the fire between them and the forest.

A soft melody floated across the water, a gentle reminder of grievances forgotten and trespasses forgiven, of hopes and of glory, of dreams both shattered and attained, of veiled illusions and of disillusionment, of birth and, yes, of death as well. For the song that played was the song of them all, the soundtrack of humanity, and if it wasn't real then certainly the effect it was having on Drew and Sera and Leviathan was visceral enough, an observable phenomenon, had anyone been around to witness it. As it was the adventurers drifted into a dreamless reverie in total isolation. Save, that is, for the old woman who hobbled up the beach path, a crooked stick aiding her steps, and sat down to warm herself by their fire.

"Oh, you romantic fools, you should not have returned," she said, shaking her head at Drew and Sera.

#

They woke long past sunrise, first Drew and then Sera, to parched mouths and matted hair and skin as salty as a goat lick. Sand stuck to their clothes and their hands and their feet, and when they tried to rinse it off in the river it turned to mud, fine silt that never seemed to quite come off no matter how much they scrubbed at it.

Leviathan was nowhere to be seen.

Drew raided the jolly boat for breakfast. Then they walked down the beach path to look for their friend and assess the island's size, first in one direction and then the other. Both sides seemed to follow the outer banks indefinitely. They returned with firewood but little else to show for t heir effort.

"At least we have food," Drew said, trying hard to sound optimistic.

Sera squeezed his hand. "And each other."

Drew's frown intensified. "About that. When Cap'n Burdock was telling her story, did you think she was talking about the sibyl... our ourselves?"

Sera took a minute to answer. "Word would've had to have gotten around pretty quick."

"I guess so. I just can't shake the feeling that I might've died too. Ever since the accident I've felt different. More confident. Like I could take on anything, because what have I got to lose?"

"I think that's called PTSD."

"Maybe."

They whiled away the afternoon building sandcastles and wading in the shallow edge of the river. In the distance Camelot's towers rose above the forest, the only reminder that they weren't alone in the universe. Twice Drew climbed the hill to see if Gabby's lean to had returned, and twice he came down disappointed.

They built a bonfire and danced around it, singing excerpts from bawdy songs and old camp classics. When the moon came out they howled at it until their lungs hurt and their throats grew hoarse.

"I know I should be worried about Levi," Drew said at one point. "But deep down, some part of me trusts the sibyl. You know? I just have this feeling that everything will work out."

"There's nothing we can do," Sera pointed out. "So why worry."

Drew didn't answer. He'd made it this far by flowing with the rhythms, usually figuratively though lately quite literally, but he hadn't always done so with grace or aplomb. Come to think of it, he'd been pushing the river as much as he'd been riding it lately. Maybe this little beach vacation would do him good.

The second day passed much like the first. Their fire was smaller that night: they'd used up all the driftwood in easy walking distance. The moon didn't come out. The air took on an ominous stillness; even the lapping river seemed to threaten to rise and disturb their sleep.

Morning came for them early. Drew blew on the fire's embers while Sera divided the remainder of their rations for breakfast. It would be their last day on the island. Either Gabby would show up or Leviathan would return, or both, or they would get into the jolly boat and paddle down the swiftly flowing river to see what fate awaited them. They squandered the last of their firewood and didn't gather more.

Finally Drew stood up and faced Sera squarely. "I feel like we're missing something," he said. "We've been sitting on this beach for three days, we've lost our friend, we've eaten all our food and can't stay much longer, and still the island is giving us nothing. Nothing! So what are we missing?"

"I know what you mean," said Sera. "It's maddening."

Drew picked up a rock and flung it into the water. "How am I supposed to prove I'm worthy of talking to the sibyl, do we have to drown ourselves again?"

Sera's gaze fell on the jolly boat. "Maybe nothing that extreme." She stood up and walked over to it. "Help me push this into the water."

"Wait, what are you doing?" said Drew. "That's our way out of here."

Sera sent him a significant look.

"Oh," he said. "Of course."

They pushed the boat into the current.

"Now we're committed," said Sera.

Hand in hand, they returned to the dying fire. Without speaking they buried it in sand until it stopped smoking. Then they walked up the hill.

A small valley lay on the other side, a lean to nestled between the dunes. Standing in front of it were Gabby and Leviathan, their hands not quite touching. The sibyl had returned to her adolescent form. The giant waved a paw.

"Took you guys long enough!" he called out.

#

CHAPTER 10

THE SIBYL'S TALE

"I don't know how long I've been here," Gabby began. She'd led them up a hidden path into the forest, to a treehouse built in a banyan nearly as old as the island itself. She ushered them in like a mother hen; the tree was so old and strong that they could all enter her house without fear of breaking its branches.

They could never have found their way back on their own, and that was before she served them a honey wine so sweet it made their ears tingle and the floor sway in rhythm to the breeze. Once her visitors were warm and fed, Gabby put a pot of cocoa on the woodstove and a pair of eyeglasses on her nose, and sat down to tell her tale.

"If you've heard stories about me they're probably true. I've crashed on this shore a thousand times and died a thousand deaths. I am the collective misfortune of the nautical realm, the earthly manifestation of Davy Jones' Locker." Gabby laughed at their faces. "I'm practicing my origin story," she explained. She took off her eyeglasses and set them aside. "No, but really. I've been here for a very long time. So long that I don't remember what it was like where I came from or have any desire to find out. I live on the island. I serve one purpose: to catch the souls who filter through and return those that need returning. But I will never return myself.

"When I arrived here I was like you when we first met, Drew Dennison. Though the occasion has slipped my mind I recall the urgent need to leave, to *go back*, to depart these lonely shores forevermore. But I was not alone.

"At first I thought the island was haunted, most likely by the shipwrecked souls with the poor fortune to end their lives here. But there were no bones, no wrecked ships, no evidence of any human presence whatsoever. So why did it feel like I was being watched? In that time there was no castle across the river, no bridge, no roughneck port town with its trappings of firewater and profiteering. I was as isolated as it was possible to be.

"And yet I couldn't shake the feeling that I was being scrutinized, judged, my eternal soul in the balance between redemption and hell. Those are antiquated concepts but I am an old woman after all.

"It was fully two months before he revealed himself. Two months of living off river water and algae, the only shelter a crude lean to I made of driftwood and vines. No fire, no companions, no hope. Each day my mind grew darker and darker, until finally I decided that I was going to take matters into my own hands."

Drew sucked in a breath. Sera placed her hand on his knee.

"I gathered the strongest vines I could find and wrapped them around a couple of river rocks using a weave I'd learned somewhere in a past life. Then I tied the vines around my waist and, holding a rock under each arm, made my way into the current. The water was colder than betrayal. I walked until my head went under, and kept walking. Then I saw my voyeur at last.

"Perhaps I should use a different word, because there was nothing sexual about him. He would've called himself a shepherd, a tender of folk; a nurturer. But in that moment he was undoubtedly my captor. I could spare you the details and simply call him a merman, or make a comparison to the sea people of the great eastern ocean. Yet I feel that would do him injustice. For Solver was not bound to the aquatic realm.

"He was waiting for me, his gargantuan arms folded across a chest that would have turned Adonis green with envy. Red hair billowed from his head and chin and the back of his arms, a kelp-like adornment that glowed with the light of his aura. From the waist down he was covered in scales, but their shimmer was such that I couldn't make out shape or form. All I know is he had a tail, because he raised it toward me and kicked so hard the vines broke and I was flung out of the water and onto the sand.

SIMULUMIS

"Then my despair turned dark, for I was truly a prisoner. And yet within that emotion lay a spark of hope, like the pearl in the center of an oyster. I had forced my captor to show himself! I resolved with all my being to see him again.

"When I sunk into the inner swamp he pulled me out. When I leapt from the highest tree he caught me. When I cut myself with a fishbone he gently bandaged my wrists. Never did he speak a word, no matter how hard I implored him.

"Eventually he came to me on his own. He would bring fillets of trout and salmon and delicacies like crab cakes and chowder. We would sit silently and eat, then I would take long walks down the beach path while he swam beside me, breaching gracefully in the cool air. I didn't need words to know he'd fallen in love. But I never forgot I was a prisoner!

"One day Solver — for that was what I called him — brought me into the forest, to this very place we are sitting now. He'd built the treehouse as a gift. I think it was his way of trying to fix me. Or affix me." She frowned at the wordplay. "As cages go, it was about as gilded as they came. I abandoned the lean to immediately. Solver caused it to be eaten up by the swamp, and in that moment of domestic bliss I was glad to see it go. I thought less and less of the affairs from my former life. They seemed more fantasy than reality, a dream I'd waken up from instead of the other way around.

"I don't know how much time passed in this way. I grew older. Solver brought me creams and ointments and potions from far off lands, but despite his tender loving care my hands and feet began to ache. My back bent forward. My left hip started clicking with each step and it became a struggle to walk down the pathway to the ocean, even with a branch for support. I knew I would have to act soon.

"Since I'd moved to the treehouse Solver had never left me alone with a sharp object. I'd held onto this byte of information through the entirety of our relationship. In every other way he had grown to trust me; I'm not even sure he would have considered this an act of mistrust. He'd anointed himself the keeper of my mental health and that was the only narrative he could see.

"The next evening, when Solver set out our plates for supper, I feigned a tremble in my arm. He made a gesture, offering to cut my meat. I accepted with a reluctant nod and dropped my steak knife in frustration. He came around the table and leaned over me, wrapping an arm around each side of my body to reach the plate. I gritted my teeth and smiled.

"Solver soaked up the praise for his heroic deed, watching my face like the narcissist he was. I let my hands think on their own. One grasped for the steak knife while the other gripped the edge of the table. When I had the knife firmly in my palm I pushed off, knocking the chair backwards into Solver. Before he knew what was happening I had spun around and buried the knife in his heart.

"He took a long time to die. I sat across the table and watched all of it, jabbing his steak knife into the wooden surface intermittently. I wasn't sure he wouldn't recover somehow and return to continue his vigil. Besides, I had nowhere to go.

"Only when he was finally and certainly dead did I allow myself to break down and cry. Then I screamed and shouted at the injustice of it all until my voice went away and I'd run out of tears. For a long time I considered burning down the treehouse with both of us in it. But I wasn't the same person who had tried to take her life so very long ago. I had, though I hate to say the words, quite literally conquered my demon. And I knew I could serve a purpose with the life I had left to live.

"So I dragged Solver outside and somehow got him down to the beach and onto a driftwood raft that had washed ashore some time ago. I built a funeral pyre and lit it before pushing the raft away from the island. And that was the last I saw of him.

"But something was happening to me. My feet didn't hurt and my hands felt strong, like they had when I'd arrived on the island and fended for myself. My spine stood straighter and the bounce returned to my step. When I looked at my reflection one calm morning the person staring back was a ten year old girl! I learned to control my age to suit my needs, and learned to ask the forest to open its pathways. When a soul washes up on the island it recedes, leaving the dunes and the lean to for the benefit of the lost. But only those who are willing to find themselves."

Gabby unfolded her hands and spread them in front of herself, an open book. "I've been here ever since."

#

The cocoa mugs were empty and the fire was dying in the woodstove. Leviathan snoozed in a corner, the walls propping him up like a teddy bear. Gabby had grown older with her tale but now she was firmly ten again, her last age of innocence.

Sera sat with Drew, holding him for comfort, though whether it was more for his or her benefit neither could say. Tears streaked both of their faces.

"I'm sorry," Drew choked out.

"Me too," said Sera.

"Thank you," Gabby said solemnly. "I told you my story because I want you to know what power can do to people. Solver may not have been a bad man, once. But when he had the power to do whatever he wanted he chose to use it against me, he chose to use me, he turned me into something I didn't choose to be! But the part that really makes me mad is how he convinced himself he was doing it *for* me. It's a strong narrative. If he'd left me alone with a knife one time, I might have let down my guard and fallen in love with him."

Sera reached across the pock-marked table with her free hand. The little girl put hers in it and smiled. "Is there something you wanted to ask me?"

Drew struggled to clear his mind. "We're trying to save the world," he began, "not just this one but the one it's modeled after. The problem is we don't know what's already been tried and what hasn't. All we know is the answer isn't disappearing into another simulation. But we can't shut it off either."

"I get that," said Gabby. "You need the people to want to be here."

"Yes!" Drew exclaimed. "Exactly!"

"If enough people elect to log out of the simulation and invest their love and energy in this world instead, you think they have the potential to heal all the wounds and injuries the planet has been dealt."

Drew nodded enthusiastically, hope momentarily sparking in his heart.

Gabby continued: "But for that to happen they need some sort of incentive, because this world is harsh and their fantasy world is full of nice things. Unfortunately mutually assured destruction does not qualify as such."

"Nobody cares," Drew translated, angry at himself for thinking there would be a simple answer.

"There may be no relatable element in the tale of a Thief, a Giant, and a Warrior Princess roaming a medieval simulation, preaching a quasi-spiritual cure for apathy," Gabby observed.

Sera caught on. "You're saying we have to model it ourselves."

Gabby shrugged.

"That can't be the answer," Drew said, pounding a fist on the table. "Just go home and live our lives?"

Gabby began clearing the dishes. "You'll wake up in the morning and all of this will be gone. The treehouse, the path, the lean to... just walk down the beach and you'll find your jolly boat grounded on the rocks. I wish you the best on your next adventure!"

Drew and Sera suddenly felt themselves growing tired, more tired than they'd been in a very long time. They laid their arms on the table and rested their heads on them.

"Wait!" cried Drew, fighting the spell. "What about Leviathan?"

#

CHAPTER 11

DOWN THE RIVER

"I'm sorry to abandon the quest," said the oversized boy, "but this is my heart's desire."

Clouds hung over the morning, like their tempers. Levi Rosen had emerged from the forest a few minutes after they woke, carrying a smorgasbord of fruits and berries and fresh coffee for breakfast. They'd eaten in silence, savoring each bite and moment before the inevitable words would have to be spoken.

Now that they had, Drew looked crestfallen. "You sure about this?"

"I've never been more certain of anything in my life," Levi said. He didn't look at Drew exactly. "You know who I am. I don't fit in, back home. It's not just the bullying. The world wasn't made for people like me. I'm better off on the island. Besides, Gabby doesn't deserve to be alone."

"Just don't turn into Solver," Sera warned.

"Oh, I won't. We talk about things."

They exchanged hugs. Then Levi took his leave, struggling up the dunes and into the overgrown undergrowth. Drew and Sera packed up what belongings they had left and bade goodbye to their campsite. Then they walked down the path.

The jolly boat was right where Gabby said it would be. She was a sibyl after all. They climbed in and shoved off from the island of lost souls. They hadn't exactly found their answer, but how many people really do?

#

They washed up in the flooded town of Delta Park, a quagmire labyrinth of girders and beams from the scattered wrecks of boats, houseboats, and houses that had never been intended to float at all. The sky refused to turn any color but gray. Sera lassoed a beam to give them time to plot a course through the minefield.

"I know why we're not in a magical fairy tale land like Oz," Drew said, scanning the jagged horizon. "This is based on the real world."

"There's a cheerful thought."

Drew dredged up a memory. "Delta was erected on top of the ruined city of Vanport, which was built during the wars so Black workers would have a place to live. When a section of railroad berm collapsed it flooded within hours. Eighteen thousand people lost their homes. My family among them."

"I'm sorry."

"Water under the bridge," he grated. Then he squinted his eyes and peered into the fog. "Hey. Isn't that the old freeway over there?"

Sera followed his gaze. "Maybe we can crawl up to it if we paddle through this."

She detached them from the beam and they eased through the muck. It was more poling than paddling. Twice the boat scraped against something and their progress was arrested. The first time Drew was able to free them by shoving his oar into the muck, but the second time it wouldn't budge. He applied leverage and the boat popped free, but not before his oar splintered under the stress.

Suddenly they were in a current. Rudderless, the boat spun about. They tried to slow their momentum, Drew in the rear slapping pylons while Sera kept them clear of obstructions.

Mud began to seep through the bottom of the boat. Drew felt it between his toes, and then around his ankles. "I don't want to alarm you," he said, trying to keep his voice level, "but-"

"I'm already alarmed!" Sera cried out. "We're in an eddy current!"

"I don't know what that means!" Drew yelled back. "But the boat's sinking!"

Sera spun around, the jolly boat remaining steady despite her maneuver. She surveyed the rising mud and Drew's appalled face in an instant. "I think we can make it to the freeway," she said, "but I won't be able to stop us when we get there. The current's too strong. We're going to have to jump."

In the old world, the one where people drove cars everywhere, a bridge had spanned the river near Delta – two bridges, eventually, for traffic grew so thick that a dedicated route was needed in both directions. The older bridge collapsed during the Great Interruption, yet another victim of civic neglect, but the slightly less old bridge – at least in Drew's reality – remained as a national monument.

Now the bridge's main vein lay before and just above them: a black asphalt snake on concrete and steel framing. The jolly boat was rushing toward it, all pretence of safety gone, a deadly race between fates: for on the far side of the freeway the eddy washed up against a jagged junkyard of old trucks and abandoned automobiles, shoved off the freeway at some point in history, their rusty frames sticking just above the water line.

"We need to still have a boat to jump off," Drew reminded her.

But Sera had turned again, for hers was the job of ensuring they sailed under the freeway and not directly into one of its pylons. And so, sparing a wistful smile for their first adventure in the bog, Drew reached down with both of his hands and began bailing mud.

Sooner than he'd have thought possible Sera called out, "Get ready!"

SIMULUMIS

They stood side by side. If they'd stayed in the front and the back they would've risked leaping at the same spot, not to mention the first jumper would rock the boat and jeopardizing the second person's balance. Better to go sideways at the same time.

Sera flung the oar into the water. One less obstruction. Drew grabbed her hand on impulse. "I'm not losing you again."

She returned the squeeze. "Not that easily."

Then they turned away from each other and prepared to jump. It wasn't a huge leap, perhaps six feet from the level of the water to the bottom rung of the guardrail. A taller man might've been able to reach it without jumping. But neither Drew nor Sera was above average height, and the sinking boat put their feet below water level... and mired in several inches of mud.

The boat reached the freeway and began to pass under it.

"Jump!" cried Sera.

They jumped. The jolly boat disappeared under the weight of the leaps, but neither Sera nor Drew had time to notice, for they were scrabbling at the guardrail for purchase, then straining to maintain it, and finally struggling to pull their mud-laden bodies up and onto the surface of the road.

"We did it," Drew gasped, flat on his back.

"Told you so," said Sera, laying an exhausted arm across his chest.

Eventually they dried out enough to start feeling uncomfortable in their river clothing, so they sat up and took stock of their surroundings.

"It's the mother slough!" Drew exclaimed.

From the freeway's small vantage they saw that the muck they'd just escaped paralleled the river's edge for a major portion of the post-metropolitan area. Beyond, smaller sloughs fingered their way between splotchy patches of trees and houses, vaguely resembling a golf course from the olden days but better suited for Leviathan sized players than Lilliputians like themselves.

"There's no place like home," Sera sighed.

"And I knew you'd make it back eventually!" a familiar voice called out.

The bedraggled adventurers turned at the sound. Roberts stood before them on the freeway's cracked asphalt, his bald head shining as much as his unfettered eyes. Behind him, the ubiquitous twin drones hovering above the road like bumblebees.

"I've been waiting for you," Roberts said. He nodded at a drone.

It buzzed forward. A tinny voice recited stoically. "Drew Dennison and Sera Hector, you are charged with the crimes of cultural subversion, terrorism, murder, and finally, obstruction of traffic."

SIMULUMIS

They were dragged to prison and ignored for twenty-four hours, which was actually pretty awesome. Their cell had a sink and towels and a bed that was just big enough for them to spoon up in together. After washing each other's faces and other body parts that needed attention, they slept for twelve straight hours. When they woke they spoke in soft murmurs and gestures, uncertain if they were being observed. Neither of them felt like rushing the inevitable. They just let the rhythms flow.

Eventually a commotion could be heard outside, and Roberts' voice sounded. "Give those kids some freaking goggles, for crying out loud!"

The door creaked open and a guard entered. He scowled at their cell, then extended a hand into it. Two pairs of virtual reality goggles lay in his palm.

Drew and Sera had composed themselves when the commotion started. Now they walked forward together. Drew nodded. Sera took a pair of goggles and he took the other. The guard turned and hurried out.

They slid the goggles on and the prison transformed into a lush suite, cleverly decorated to suggest that they *could* walk out into the hallway and leave, but it was so comfy here that nobody should really want to.

Then Roberts stepped into the hallway, slamming the door on his retinue with a grunt. With deliberate slowness he turned to scowl at his captives.

"You meddling kids have caused me no end of trouble."

"Hey, Teach," Sera said, a wicked smile playing across her lips. "Or should I call you Founder?"

"You know who I am," Roberts sighed. "That's awkward."

"Oh, we know much more than that."

"It doesn't matter," he said. "These charges are pretty severe, except the obstruction of traffic; you can probably get off with a fine for that. I'd usually just have a page take care of the details for your execution. None of that's why I came to see you myself."

"Did you say execution?" Drew's eyes widened theatrically.

"Hey, you plotted to overthrow the dominant paradigm of the realm! What am I supposed to do, offer you jobs?"

"Touché. Please continue," Drew conceded, a touch quickly.

"Thanks," Roberts said, frowning in suspicion. "Well, you're very public figures of infamy now, and that complicates matters. I can't just kill you off behind the chemical sheds. The people want a circus."

Drew risked a glance at Sera.

"If you know who I am, you know the power I have over your world," Roberts continued. "I could wipe it out of existence with less effort that it takes to wipe my butt. However, I'm not a monster. I want to offer you a deal.

"I know this world is as real to you as my own is to me. Your families, your loved ones; all of them will perish if I'm forced to flip the switch and shut off Simulumis. You don't want that to happen, do you?"

"Just tell us your offer," Sera grated.

Roberts sighed. "Very well. I won't erase your world out of existence if you give the people what they want."

#

CHAPTER 12

COLISEUM

"Step right up, ladies and gentlefolk, and get your tickets for the show of a lifetime, get them before they're gone, that's right, I said the show of a lifetime! Coming at you tonight only, we have the live and very public execution of the infamous, the insipid, the entirely un-inspirational elf turned preacher, Drew the Thief! At his side will be the lovely, the luscious, the soon-to-be late Sera: Warrior Princess! But she's not just a sidekick, folks, no: she's the Juliet to his Romeo, the Bonnie to his Clyde, the Katniss to his... well, I didn't really understand those movies, but you get the point: we've got star-crossed lovers in the house!"

The old Memorial Coliseum was packed with people as diverse as the parade in Balal. In fact they'd brought in the barker and, it seemed, the rest of the market-goers from the pocket universe as well. A very unhappy horde of orcs had claimed the front row, waving protest signs and booing.

SIMULUMIS

The smallest had a hunchback. In the royal booth Roberts sat beside a girl that must've been Vinge.

It was a lively crowd, and as Drew and Sera watched the pregame via live feed from their cell it was hard not to get the slightest tinge of stage fright. This was their most important show, the culmination of all their efforts. Their performance would have to be top notch, each line delivered with the impact of a blade. They went over the routine until their words turned to gibberish and their jaws vibrated so hard they had to rub them with their hands and splash water on their faces. They spent some time kissing.

"If this doesn't go well," Drew began at one point, but Sera put a finger on his lips.

"Just flow with the rhythm."

The first bout was a grudge match between a troll and its mate, neither of whom could ever recall the other's name or birthday. They fought with plastic nunchaku and wore helmets, and after one of them — nobody could tell which, nor cared — bashed the other sufficiently on the head, they both retired to the bar amidst the cheers and jeers of the crowd.

Next came a MMA bout between a boxer and a dancing faun. It was over quickly and the crowd booed and called for blood.

Roberts obliged. An ogre took on a squadron and tore them apart. Then it fought a centaur with a crossbow who nearly managed to kill it while galloping in circles, but the ogre got in a lucky swipe and broke his leg. The third fight was hardly a fair one at all, for the ogre was mortally wounded; yet it fought admirably and died to a roar of approval. Its foe, a haughty goliath wearing a ram skull helmet, strutted around the arena daring anyone to fight him.

Sera clenched her hands into fists and scowled.

"Patience, my lady."

Yet it seemed the crowd was as impatient as she, for they began to chant the names of the damned; or at least hers, it being obvious which of them was the fighter. Though nothing about Drew the Thief rang mnemonically, so it may have been that. In any case Roberts read the room, and sooner than the dynamic duo could say break a leg – no offense to the centaur – they were summoned from their cell and escorted down the long tunnel into the bright lights of stardom.

#

"In the north corner, weighing in at three hundred and thirty-three back-breaking pounds, from Tuscaloosa Alabama, our champion, the indomitable Mordecai Manson!"

Ram skull swaggered about the arena, showing off his prowess for his adulating fans. They screamed and hooted and stomped their feet until the vibrations threatened to collapse the ancient building. Then the barker waved them to silence, though it took a full two minutes for his voice to be heard, PA system and all.

"And in the south corner, weighing in with a philosophy nobody wants to listen to, from the depths of the swamp and a direct nemesis of our Lord Roberts himself, our challenger, the Warrior Princess Sera Hector!"

For a long second nothing happened. The coliseum grew silent. Then Sera sauntered through the tunnel's exit like she hadn't a care in the world. Her sword was sheathed and her shield hung loosely from her arm. The noonday sun reflected off the goggles in her eyes. She was whistling.

The crowd went wild.

Mordecai roared in anger at her entrance, furious to be upstaged. He raised his sword, already drawn and poised, and rushed at his opponent. Sera dodged his initial attack, goose-stepping to the side. As Mordecai turned he swung his broadsword in a death arc that would've severed her head had she been where he was expecting her to be. Instead Sera had nimbly withdrawn to the center of the arena and was waiting for him, hands on hips and motionless.

Mordecai snarled and advanced. As the duelists came together and the sounds of steel on steel rang out above the din of the spectators' cries, Drew slipped unnoticed out of the tunnel and crept toward the barker's booth.

They were fighting in earnest now, blows glancing off shields and sparks flying as their swords clashed together. Sera was quicker than Mordecai, which balanced his size and made the fight fair, if not equal. And yet their strategy was the same: attack with sheer force and destroy everything in their path. Round and round they went, neither able to penetrate the other's guard, a stalemate in the making.

Then Mordecai telegraphed his charge and Sera leapt into the air, bringing her shield down on his helmet with a mighty blow. The goliath was unfazed, yet when they turned to face each other his ram skull was cracked, hanging over his left eye like a premonition. He flung it aside and leered. Blood dripped down his forehead.

Sera poised for his attack. But her shield hung limply from her arm, and as Mordecai charged she struggled to free herself from its straps. At the last moment she sliced them with her sword and rolled aside, the wind from her opponent's broadsword ruffling her hair.

The duelists circled again. A hush fell over the stadium. Every eye followed the action with the focus of obsession, a mob hinged in the moment, their collective spirit holding the power to change the world.

It was into this vacuum that Drew spoke. "My fellow humans!"

His voice boomed from the PA system and his face leapt onto the overhead game screen, goggles aglow. A drum beat started looping. The barker was tapping at a synthesizer, his head nodding in rhythm, a shit-eating grin splitting his face.

"There's so much I want to tell you, but why would you believe a *Loomie*?"

Boom boom clap! Parry, thrust, repeat.

"My name is Andrew Dennison and I'm sixteen years old."

Boom boom clap! Clang! Bash! Crash!

"Do you want to see me die today?"

The crowd rumbled in response, but it was a confused rumble. Those who were about to die should be saluting, not narrating the show.

"My girlfriend's not going to lose," Drew said confidently, "and you all know who she's fighting next. Is that what you want?"

The crowd was muttering now. Was he asking for mercy?

Chicka chicka boom boom. Lunge, parry, thrust.

"This is what the founders made the internet to keep from happening, but hey, it's your party! The only thing I ask is, if I die and respawn, don't start a church in my name!"

"Jesus Christ!" someone in the audience yelled. "Shut up!"

Faces turned to the royal booth, looking for their overlords to put an end to the tomfoolery. But Roberts just watched, an alert and interested expression on his face. Vinge was sub-vocalizing rapidly, as if she was an announcer herself.

Boom! Crash!

"I'm going to take off my goggles now," Drew said, "Then I'm going to step away from this microphone and walk into the arena. If you want my death on your hands all you have to do is sit there and let it happen."

#

Andrew Dennison walked into the arena, a tiny figure on a huge game screen. He was barefoot and his synthetic jeans were tattered and ragged. His shirt, an old Grant High commemorative tee, looked more like the spreading slough than a body covering.

The beat changed. Now it was all high hat, growing toward a crescendo.

As Andrew approached the duelists, Sera let loose with a flurry of blows. Mordecai was forced to his knees. His sword faltered, then was whisked out of his hand. Sera hollered triumphantly and cocked her elbow, her sword quivering horizontally, poised for the kill.

Mordecai gave up. He visibly wilted and shook in terror. "Please don't kill me," he begged, "I have a wife and three kids. They're depending on me!"

Sera handed Andrew her sword. Then she removed her goggles, and when she took them off the entire stadium sucked in its breath. The warrior princess was even more striking in real life than her avatar. This wasn't to say she was simply a creature of beauty, a dainty lass to objectify, no: the real Sera Hector was as dirty and beaten up as Andrew, but her spirit shone through her confidence and her bearing.

She turned to the crowd, and when she spoke her voice projected just as loud as when Andrew had used the PA. "There is no big red button!" she said. "We can't go back to the way it was before. We can only go forward. We can only keep trying. We may still get there, but not by *forcing* it on anybody." She held up her goggles. "Nobody can take these off for you. You have to do it yourself."

Sera took back her sword and dropped it on the ground in front of Mordecai.

"What's it going to be then?" she yelled, staring the crowd down.

The jeopardy theme song began playing.

On the last note, the orc horde rose up. They threw down their protest signs and, as a unit, removed their goggles. Their demon features withered but they were still undoubtedly old and decrepit.

The Balal crew were a different story. Some got on the bandwagon but just as many sat there, indifferent, waiting to see how things shook out. Others were vehemently upset. They yelled and booed and accused Drew of robbing them of their circus. A few of the bolder hooligans leaped into the arena.

Mordecai got to his feet. He picked up the discarded sword and looked Sera in the eye. "I'll follow your lead, but let me take care of them first."

With a primal scream, the goliath rushed the insurrectionists. He only had to fight one before the rest fled in terror. Witnessing their champion's turn of heart, the audience hit a sort of tipping point. People began ripping off their goggles. Mothers and fathers and sisters and brothers, big and small folk and people of all sizes and nationalities, persuasions, genders, and beliefs appeared in the seats that had until seconds before been occupied by fairies and trolls and other mythological beings. Everyone looked around in a daze, as if it had been a very long time since they'd seen another human being. Confused hubbub filled the stadium.

Andrew Dennison turned to the barker, who saluted him and took off his goggles. He looked exactly the same underneath. Then he tossed Andrew the microphone.

"Go live your lives," Andrew said. "It won't be easy. You'll make mistakes. You'll make your own lenses and have to take them off again and again, but the important thing is to keep trying! That's the quest. It's not about leveling up. It's about staying level."

He held the microphone out. Then he dropped it.

Sera patted him on the back. "Nice sermon, dude. And way to end it with the wordplay! You'll be leading quests in the real world soon enough."

"I think they used to call that politics."

#

CHAPTER 13

DEUCED MACHINE

The mess of discarded goggles outside the coliseum was a sight to see. Drew and Sera, the last to leave the stadium, stepped through the litter ruefully.

"There's gonna be a lot of people regretting this in the morning," Drew said.

Sera shook her head. "You know they can just put them back on."

"*We* know that," Drew agreed. Then he shrugged. "They'll figure it out soon enough. It's not our place to police anyone. If it happens again it happens again."

"They're not the same people they used to be," Sera pointed out. "Maybe they'll make different choices next time."

"It's always possible."

Mordecai approached with his family in tow. He was overweight and sweating, but seemed happy with the way his genes fit. He introduced his wife and children and thanked them again for sparing his life.

"Everything looks so different," he kept saying.

"Go forth," Sera told Mordecai, "and tell everyone what happened today."

They held hands as they walked through the city. It was truly a beautiful day: the fog was lifting and hope filled the air. Birds flew through the slough fingers that edged the grassy streets. Buildings appeared that may have been there since the nineteenth century.

They reached the old ball park and walked through it deliberately. Drew pointed out where he'd first been approached by Roberts. There was no evidence anything untoward had ever happened.

"I guess it's best this way."

Sera studied her companion. "You still have questions."

"My father did. He never got any sort of an explanation. A grand summary to justify his suffering."

"Okay," said Sera, "how about this?" She held up her hands to box in her face like an old television screen. "Arthur never got to meet his God, but that's a good thing because he would've been disappointed. Either God had the power to make things better and chose not to use it, or he was just another schmuck leveling up like you and me; and in any case it would have changed nothing."

"Or," said Drew, making his own box, "God *was* the machine all along."

Sera dropped her TV. "A literal deus ex machina. I hate that so much."

"Well, how do you feel about living in a simulation?"

She gave him a little smile. "I don't have anything to compare it to."

By the time they reached Drew's street the city was back to normal, at least the parts they could see. People went about their business as if nothing had happened, and for many of them it hadn't. Not yet.

Finally they arrived at his house and stopped on the front porch, awkwardly shy of a sudden, though they faced one another and gripped both hands tightly. This was not a part of the quest either had prepared for.

Drew gathered all the lessons he'd learned from their mad adventure, made the commitment, and took action.

He said, "do you want to come inside and meet my mother?"

#

EPILOGUE

In the deepest dungeon of the most isolated prison on the planet, Arthur Dennison sat in a meditative half-lotus position, his palms resting gently on his knees, his eyes lightly closed. A scruffy beard grew on his chin. In one corner a wooden bucket attracted flies. In another lay a thin pallet of straw. The only break in the ubiquitous stonework that made up his cell was the doorway, a six inch thick iron behemoth with a tiny window through which a ray of LED light emerged from the corridor where he'd first come to the prison. Where that light hit the wall Arthur had scrawled a series of lines, ostensibly to mark the days – or the meals, or when his bucket was removed; whatever method of tracking time was available to one removed from the diurnal rhythms of the planet.

Such an event was nigh, for the distant scrabbling of lock in key caused Arthur to open an eye and train it on the door, just below the window. Staring at the light itself caused a blindness he'd rather avoid. Footsteps echoed in the hall. Then the light dimmed as someone put their head in the viewing window.

"Hello, grandson," the voice said.

Arthur opened his second eye to scrutinize the visitor. "You!"

"Bit of a surprise, is it? Thought you had it all figured out?" Vinge gave him a sad little smile.

"But…"

"Why would I give you the backdoor but refuse to speak to you? Why would I threaten to blink your world out of existence? Think about it, Art. I don't even have a kid!"

"You haven't done those things yet," Arthur said. "You don't approve of your own future actions."

"Approval is irrelevant. Results are all that matters."

They stared at each other through the dimly lit window, one avatar to another: the adult grandchild of a future that had not yet happened and the young woman who held the power to prevent it from coming to be.

"How did Andrew's plan work out? I am still alive, it would seem."

"So it would," Vinge agreed.

"Does that mean we made it? Saved the human race?"

"Time will tell." A real smile broke her lips, the first occasion Arthur had seen such an event. "It was a bold move, using himself as a fulcrum. He did the family proud."

"Am I free to go then?"

SIMULUMIS

Vinge let out a lengthy sigh. "These people are just coming to terms with the fact that their wholesale immersion in a fantasy land is in large part responsible for the sickness of their world. They are not ready for the leader of a terrorist organization who claims that world is not real to walk amongst them."

"But I wouldn't–"

"I'm sorry," Vinge said, cutting him off, "it's out of my hands. The decision has been made."

Arthur gave a curt nod. "You already know what happens."

"What's most likely to," she corrected. "Getting Simulumis to this point at all had a very low probability. It took far more of our resources than we can afford to expend indefinitely. Now we need to dedicate them to building a plausible, self-sustaining future. In the real world."

"As modeled by ours."

"Granted."

"What happens to the other simulations? The ones that fail?"

Vinge regarded her elderly grandson for the space of several seconds before she spoke. "There are no other simulations, Arthur. We only have the processing power to run one at a time."

#

The massive iron door swung open. The drones floated in, their buzzing motors creating tiny whirlwinds of dust in the stale air. They positioned themselves on either side of Arthur. Vinge stood in the doorway, a torch in one hand.

Arthur faced his captor. "Where are you taking me?"

Vinge gestured at the drones. They nudged Arthur forward. The procession left the cell and moved down the hallway, Vinge in the lead. They came to a door that opened into an elevator of sorts. Arthur waited patiently as Vinge navigated, or dialed in their destination, or did whatever it was she needed to with the keypad on the wall.

Then the door opened again. At the gentle urging of the drones Arthur stepped out. And gasped in surprise. They stood in the foyer of the black castle. Before them rose the spiral staircase to the belfry. Pacing to and fro between the dining hall and the guest quarters and the other rooms that made up the stark mansion's interior were orc-like figures, all of whom stopped in their tracks to gawk at the sudden appearance of the interlopers.

"Artie!" cried one of the orcs.

"My lord, my liege," said Janaway, dropping to one knee awkwardly.

"They have elected to join you in banishment," Vinge explained. "One of my drones will remain as well, to ensure you do not regain access to my future self's backdoor.

This is the best deal I could get. My colleague wanted to respawn you."

"Kill me, you mean."

"Is the loss of memory the death of the soul?" Vinge directed a look at Janaway, who shrugged in confusion.

"Do programs have souls?" Arthur shot back. "I seem to recall that being an unresolved matter."

"The human soul has yet to be proven in any conclusive manner," Janaway piped up. "If that helps at all."

"Whatever!" Vinge threw her arms in the air. "I prevailed in saving your life, if that's what you want to call it, for one reason. And that is the extremely unlikely event – one tenth of one percent, in fact – that human survival requires a villain. You're our wild card.

"You will spend the rest of your lives here. There is food and drink for the seven of you to live in comfort. But if the bulb in your belfry ever lights up, you will know the world has need of the Lumis culture once again."

#

Vinge made one more stop before she logged out of the simulation. Rendering herself invisible to everyone, even those people who'd removed their goggles, she slipped into Drew Dennison's house and entered his bedroom. She watched over the sleeping form of her great-grandson, a lone tear running down her cheek. He was only a few years younger than herself. How much had been demanded of him already!

Vinge knew something of demands. It was she who had proposed the future simulation; she who had spurred the congress to action when all seemed lost; she who had held the delegation together by the thinnest of threads as model after model failed, until they'd finally been forced to intervene in their own experiment in order to produce the results that would convince the factions to keep from killing each other for another day.

She leaned over and kissed Drew's forehead.

"Rest up, boy," she whispered. "You're gonna need it."

#

END OF LEVEL ONE

ACKNOWLEDGEMENTS

A huge thanks to Cypria Dionese for introducing me to the simulation theory. Big thanks to first draft readers and listeners including Sarah Moen and family, Marina Menegol, Abdiel Jayne, Alix Brooks, and Josh Humbert. Thank you dad for never going out for a cigarette and not coming back. Thank you mom for always telling it like you see it. Thanks to Ann Hymas for sharing the journey of parenthood. Thanks to Frank Munden for encouraging me to keep writing. Thanks to everyone who's kept me afloat by supporting my woodworking business. Thanks to (the unprecedented) Magpie for the cover art. Special shout out to Joanna Martelles for encouraging me to put myself out there.

Tip of the hat to Grandpa Joe from Bruce Sterling's Zeitgeist. Big respect to Seveneves and Maddaddam by Neal Stephenson and Margaret Atwood, respectively.

This book was originally copyrighted under the pen name Ned Rage Garden.